THE TURKEY THE RIDERS

THE TURKEYFEATHER RIDERS

A Western Quintet

LOUIS L'AMOUR

edited by

JON TUSKA

SAGEBRUSH
Large Print Westerns

First published in Great Britain by ISIS Publishing Ltd.
First published in the United States by Circle (V) Westerns

Published in Large Print 2013 by ISIS Publishing Ltd.,
7 Centremead, Osney Mead, Oxford OX2 0ES
by arrangement with
The Golden West Literary Agency

British Library Cataloguing in Publication Data
L'Amour, Louis, 1908–1988
 The turkeyfeather riders: a western quintet.
 1. Western stories.
 2. Large type books.
 I. Title II. Tuska, Jon.
 813.5'2–dc23

ISBN 978–0–7531–9124–8 (pb)

Printed and bound in Great Britain by
T. J. International Ltd., Padstow, Cornwall

Acknowledgments

"West is Where the Heart Is" by Louis L'Amour first appeared in *Popular Western* (4/51). Copyright © 1951 by Better Publications, Inc. Copyright not renewed.

"Fork Your Own Broncs" under the byline Jim Mayo first appeared in *Thrilling Ranch Stories* (5/47). Copyright © 1947 by Standard Magazines, Inc. Copyright not renewed.

"Riding for the Brand" under the byline Jim Mayo first appeared in *Thrilling Western* (9/48). Copyright © 1948 by Standard Magazines, Inc. Copyright not renewed.

"Four Card Draw" under the byline Jim Mayo first appeared in *Giant Western* (2/51). Copyright © 1951 by Best Publications, Inc. Copyright not renewed.

"The Turkeyfeather Riders" under the byline Jim Mayo first appeared in *West* (5/49). Copyright © 1949 by Better Magazines, Inc. Copyright not renewed.

Table of Contents

Introduction

by Jon Tuska

Louis Dearborn LaMoore (1908–1988) was born in Jamestown, North Dakota. He left home at fifteen and subsequently held a wide variety of jobs although he worked mostly as a merchant seaman. From his earliest youth, L'Amour had a love of verse. His first published work was a poem, "The Chap Worth While", appearing when he was eighteen years old in his former hometown's newspaper, the *Jamestown Sun*. It is the only poem from his early years that he left out of SMOKE FROM THIS ALTAR, which appeared in 1939 from Lusk Publishers in Oklahoma City, a book which L'Amour published himself; however, this poem is reproduced in THE LOUIS L'AMOUR COMPANION (Andrews and McMeel, 1992) edited by Robert Weinberg. L'Amour wrote poems and articles for a number of small circulation arts magazines all through the early 1930s and, after hundreds of rejection slips, finally had his first story accepted, "Anything for a Pal" in *True Gang Life* (10/35). He returned in 1938 to live with his family where they had settled in Choctaw, Oklahoma, determined to make writing his career. He wrote a fight story bought by Standard Magazines that year and became acquainted with editor Leo Margulies who was to play an important rôle later in L'Amour's life. "The Town No Guns Could Tame" in *New Western* (3/40) was his first published Western story.

During the Second World War L'Amour was drafted and ultimately served with the U.S. Army Transportation Corps in Europe. However, in the two years before he was shipped out, he managed to write a great many adventure stories for Standard Magazines. The first story he published in 1946, the year of his discharge, was a Western, "Law of the Desert Born" in *Dime Western* (4/46). A call to Leo Margulies resulted in L'Amour's agreeing to write Western stories for the various Western pulp magazines published by Standard Magazines, a third of which appeared under the byline Jim Mayo, the name of a character in L'Amour's earlier adventure fiction. The proposal for L'Amour to write new Hopalong Cassidy novels came from Margulies who wanted to launch *Hopalong Cassidy's Western Magazine* to take advantage of the popularity William Boyd's old films and new television series were enjoying with a new generation. Doubleday & Company agreed to publish the pulp novelettes in hard cover books. L'Amour was paid $500 a story, no royalties, and he was assigned the house name Tex Burns. L'Amour read Clarence E. Mulford's books about the Bar-20 and based his Hopalong Cassidy on Mulford's original creation. Only two issues of the magazine appeared before it ceased publication. Doubleday felt that the Hopalong character had to appear exactly as William Boyd did in the films and on television and thus even the first two novels had to be revamped to meet with this requirement prior to publication in book form.

L'Amour's first Western novel under his own byline was WESTWARD THE TIDE (World's Work, 1950). It was rejected by every American publisher to which it was submitted. World's Work paid a flat £75 without royalties for British Empire rights in perpetuity. L'Amour sold his first Western short story to a slick magazine a year later, "The Gift of Cochise" in *Collier's* (7/5/52). Robert Fellows and John Wayne purchased screen rights to this story from L'Amour for $4,000 and James Edward Grant, one of Wayne's favorite screenwriters, developed a script from it, changing L'Amour's Ches Lane to Hondo Lane. L'Amour retained the right to novelize Grant's screenplay, which differs substantially from his short story, and he was able to get an endorsement from Wayne to be used as a blurb, stating that HONDO was the finest Western Wayne had ever read. HONDO (Fawcett Gold Medal, 1953) by Louis L'Amour was released on the same day as the film, HONDO (Warner, 1953), with a first printing of 320,000 copies.

With SHOWDOWN AT YELLOW BUTTE (Ace, 1953) by Jim Mayo, L'Amour began a series of short Western novels for Don Wollheim that could be doubled with other short novels by other authors in Ace Publishing's paperback two-fers. Advances on these were $800 and usually the author never earned any royalties. HELLER WITH A GUN (Fawcett Gold Medal, 1955) was the first of a series of original Westerns L'Amour had agreed to write under his own name following the success for Fawcett of HONDO. L'Amour wanted even this early to have his Western novels published in hard cover editions. He expanded "Guns of the Timberland" by Jim Mayo in *West* (9/50) for GUNS OF THE TIMBERLANDS (Jason Press, 1955), a hard cover Western for which he was paid an advance of $250. Another novel for Jason Press followed and then SILVER CAÑON (Avalon Books, 1956) for Thomas Bouregy & Company. These were basically lending library publishers and the books seldom earned much money above the small advances paid.

The great turn in L'Amour's fortunes came about because of problems Saul David was having with his original paperback Westerns program at Bantam Books. Fred Glidden had been signed to a contract to produce two original paperback Luke Short Western novels a year for an advance of $15,000 each. It was a long-term contract but, in the first ten years of it, Fred only wrote six novels. Literary agent Marguerite Harper then persuaded Bantam that Fred's brother, Jon, could help fulfill the contract and Jon was signed for eight Peter Dawson Western novels. When Jon died suddenly before completing even one book for Bantam, Harper managed to engage a ghost writer at the Disney studios to write these eight "Peter Dawson" novels, beginning with THE SAVAGES (Bantam, 1959). They proved inferior to anything Jon had ever written and what sales they had seemed to be due only to the Peter Dawson name.

Saul David wanted to know from L'Amour if *he* could deliver two Western novels a year. L'Amour said he could, and he did. In fact, by 1962 this number was increased to three original paperback novels a year. The first L'Amour novel to appear under the Bantam contract was RADIGAN (Bantam, 1958). It seemed to me after I read all of the Western stories L'Amour ever wrote in preparation for my essay, "Louis L'Amour's Western Fiction" in A VARIABLE HARVEST (McFarland, 1990), that by the time L'Amour wrote "Riders of the Dawn" in *Giant Western* (6/51), the short novel he later expanded to form SILVER CAÑON, that he had almost burned out on the Western story, and this was years before his fame, wealth, and tremendous sales figures. He had developed seven basic plot situations in his pulp Western stories and he used them over and over again in writing his original paperback Westerns. FLINT (Bantam, 1960), considered by many to be one of L'Amour's better efforts, is basically a reprise of the range war plot which, of the seven, is the one L'Amour used most often. L'Amour's hero, Flint, knows about a hide-out in the badlands (where, depending on the story, something is hidden: cattle, horses, outlaws, etc.). Even certain episodes within his basic plots are repeated again and again. Flint scales a sharp V in a cañon wall to escape a tight spot as Jim Gatlin had before him in L'Amour's "The Black Rock Coffin Makers" in *.44 Western* (2/50) and many a L'Amour hero would again.

Basic to this range war plot is the villain's means for crowding out the other ranchers in a district. He brings in a giant herd that requires all the available grass and forces all the smaller ranchers out of business. It was this same strategy Bantam used in marketing L'Amour. *All* of his Western titles were continuously kept in print. Independent distributors were required to buy titles in lots of 10,000 copies if they wanted access to other Bantam titles at significantly discounted prices. In time L'Amour's paperbacks forced almost every one else off the racks in the Western sections. L'Amour himself comprised the other half of this successful strategy. He dressed up in cowboy outfits, traveled about the country in a motor home visiting with independent distributors, taking them to dinner and charming them, making them personal friends. He promoted himself at every available opportunity. L'Amour insisted that he was telling the stories of the people who had made America a great nation and he appealed to patriotism as much as to commercialism in his rhetoric.

His fiction suffered, of course, stories written hurriedly and submitted in their first draft and published as he wrote them. A character would have a rifle in his hand, a model not yet invented in the period in which the story was set, and when he crossed a street the rifle would vanish without explanation. A scene would begin in a saloon and suddenly the setting would be a hotel dining room. Characters would die once and, a few pages later, die again. An old man for most of a story would turn out to be in his twenties.

Once when we were talking and Louis had showed me his topographical maps and his library of thousands of volumes which he claimed he used for research, he asserted that, if he claimed there was a rock in a road at a certain point in a story, his readers knew that if they went to that spot they would find the rock just as he described it. I told him that might be so but I personally was troubled by the many inconsistencies in his stories. Take LAST STAND AT PAPAGO WELLS (Fawcett Gold Medal, 1957). Five characters are killed during an Indian raid. One of the surviving characters emerges from seclusion after the attack and counts *six* corpses.

"I'll have to go back and count them again," L'Amour said, and smiled. "But, you know, I don't think the people who read my books would really care."

All of this notwithstanding, there are many fine, and some spectacular, moments in Louis L'Amour's Western fiction. I think he was at his best in the shorter forms, especially his magazine stories, and the two best stories he ever wrote appeared in the 1950s, "The Gift of Cochise" early in the decade and "War Party" in *The Saturday Evening Post* (6/59). The latter was later expanded by L'Amour to serve as the opening chapters for BENDIGO SHAFTER (Dutton, 1979). That book is so poorly structured that Harold Kuebler, senior editor at Doubleday & Company to whom it was first offered, said he would not publish it unless L'Amour undertook extensive revisions. This L'Amour refused to do and, eventually, Bantam started a hard cover publishing program to accommodate him when no other hard cover publisher proved willing to accept his books as he wrote them. Yet "War Party" possesses several of the characteristics in purest form which I suspect, no matter how diluted they ultimately would become, account in largest measure for the loyal following Louis L'Amour won from his readers: the young male narrator who is in the process of growing into manhood and who is evaluating other human beings and his own experiences; a resourceful frontier woman who has beauty as well as fortitude; a strong male character who is single and hence marriageable; and the powerful, romantic, strangely compelling vision of the American West which invests L'Amour's Western fiction and makes it such a delightful escape from the cares of a later time — in this author's words from this story, that "big country needing big men and women to live in it" and where there was no place for "the frightened or the mean."

West Is Where the Heart Is

Jim London lay face down in the dry prairie grass, his body pressed tightly against the ground. Heat, starvation, and exhaustion had taken a toll of his lean, powerful body, and, although light-headed from their accumulative effects, he still grasped the fact that to survive he must not be seen.

Hot sun blazed upon his back, and in his nostrils was the stale, sour smell of clothes and body long unwashed. Behind him lay days of dodging Comanche war parties and sleeping on the bare ground behind rocks or under bushes. He was without weapons or food, and it had been nine hours since he had tasted water, and that was only dew he had licked from leaves.

The screams of the dying rang in his ears, amid the sounds of occasional shots and the shouts and war cries of the Indians. From a hill almost five miles away he had spotted the white canvas tops of the Conestoga wagons and had taken a course that would intercept them. And then, in the last few minutes before he could reach their help, the Comanches had hit the wagon train.

From the way the attack went, a number of the Indians must have been bedded down in the tall grass, keeping out of sight, and then, when the train was passing, they sprang for the drivers of the teams. The strategy was perfect, for there was then no chance of the wagon train making its circle. The lead wagons did swing, but two other teamsters were dead and another was fighting for his life, and their wagons could not be turned. The two lead wagons found themselves isolated from the last four and were hit hard by at least twenty Indians. The wagon whose driver was fighting turned over in the tall grass at the edge of a ditch, and the driver was killed.

Within twenty minutes after the beginning of the attack, the fighting was over and the wagons looted, and the Indians were riding away, leaving behind them only dead and butchered oxen, the scalped and mutilated bodies of the drivers, and the women who were killed or who had killed themselves.

Yet Jim London did not move. This was not his first crossing of the plains or his first encounter with Indians. He had fought Comanches before, as well as Kiowas, Apaches, Sioux, and Cheyennes. Born on the Oregon Trail, he had later been a teamster on the Santa Fe. He knew better than to move now. He knew that an Indian or two might come back to look for more loot.

The smoke of the burning wagons bit at his nostrils, yet he waited. An hour had passed before he let himself move, and then it was only to inch to the top of the hill, where from behind a tuft of bunch grass he surveyed the scene before him.

No living thing stirred near the wagons. Slow tendrils of smoke lifted from blackened timbers and wheel spokes. Bodies lay scattered about, grotesque in

10

attitudes of tortured death. For a long time he studied the scene below, and the surrounding hills. And then he crawled over the skyline and slithered downhill through the grass, making no more visible disturbance than a snake or a coyote.

This was not the first such wagon train he had come upon, and he knew there was every chance that he would find food among the ruins as well as water, perhaps even overlooked weapons. Indians looted hastily and took the more obvious things, usually scattering food and wasting what they could not easily carry away.

Home was still more than two hundred miles away, and the wife he had not seen in four years would be waiting for him. In his heart, he knew she would be waiting. During the war the others had scoffed at him.

"Why, Jim, you say yourself she don't even know where you're at. She probably figures you're dead. No woman can be expected to wait that long. Not for a man she never hears of and when she's in a good country for men and a bad one for women."

"She'll wait. I know Jane."

"No man knows a woman that well. No man could. You say yourself you come East with a wagon train in 'Sixty-One. Now it's 'Sixty-Four. You been in the war, you been wounded, you ain't been home, nor heard from her, nor she from you. Worst of all, she was left on a piece of ground with only a cabin built, no ground broke, no close up neighbors. I'll tell you, Jim, you're crazy. Come, go to Mexico with us."

"No," he had said stubbornly. "I'll go home. I'll go back to Jane. I came East after some fixings for her, after some stock for the ranch, and I'll go home with what I set out after."

"You got any young 'uns?" The big sergeant had been skeptical.

"Nope. I sure ain't, but I wish I did. Only," he had added, "maybe I have. Jane, she was expecting, but had a time to go when I left. I only figured to be gone four months."

"And you been gone four years?" The sergeant had shook his head. "Forget her, Jim, and come with us. Nobody would deny she was a good woman. From what you tell of her, she sure was, but she's been alone and no doubt figures you're dead. She'll be married again, maybe with a family."

Jim London had shaken his head. "I never took up with no other woman, and Jane wouldn't take up with any other man. I'm going home."

He had made a good start. He had saved nearly every dime of pay, and he did some shrewd buying and trading when the war was over. He started West with a small but good train, and he had two wagons with six head of mules to the wagon, knowing the mules would sell better in New Mexico than would oxen. He had six cows and a yearling bull, some pigs, chickens, and utensils. He was a proud man when he looked over his outfit, and he hired two boys with the train to help him with the extra wagon and the stock.

Comanches hit them before they were well started. They killed two men, and one woman and stampeded some stock. The wagon train continued, and at the forks of Little Creek they struck again, in force this time, and only Jim London came out of it alive. All his outfit was gone, and he escaped without weapons, food, or water.

He lay flat in the grass at the edge of the burned spot. Again he studied the hills, and then he eased forward and got to his feet. The nearest wagon was upright, and smoke was still rising from it. The wheels were partly burned, the box badly charred, and the interior smoking. It was still too hot to touch.

He crouched near the front wheel and studied the situation, avoiding the bodies. No weapons were in sight, but he had scarcely expected any. There had been nine wagons. The lead wagons were thirty or forty yards off, and the three wagons whose drivers had been attacked were bunched in the middle with one overturned. The last four, near one of which he was crouched, had burned further than the others.

Suddenly he saw a dead horse lying at one side with a canteen tied to the saddle. He crossed to it at once, and, tearing the canteen loose, he rinsed his mouth with water. Gripping himself tight against drinking, he rinsed his mouth again and moistened his cracked lips. Only then did he let a mere swallow trickle down his parched throat.

Resolutely he put the canteen down in the shade and went through the saddle pockets. It was a treasure trove. He found a good-size chunk of almost iron-hard brown sugar, a half dozen biscuits, a chunk of jerky wrapped in paper, and a new plug of chewing tobacco.

Putting these things with the canteen, he unfastened the slicker from behind the saddle and added that to the pile.

Wagon by wagon he searched, always alert to the surrounding country and at times leaving the wagons to observe the plain from a hilltop. It was quite dark before he was finished. Then he took his first good drink, for he had allowed himself only nips during the remainder of the day. He took his drink, and then ate a biscuit, and chewed a piece of the jerky. With his hunting knife he shaved a little of the plug tobacco and made a cigarette by rolling it in paper, the way the Mexicans did.

Every instinct warned him to be away from the place by daylight, and, as much as he disliked leaving the bodies as they were, he knew it would be folly to bury them. If the Indians passed that way again, they would find them buried and would immediately be on his trail.

Crawling along the edge of the taller grass near the depression where the wagon had tipped over, he stopped suddenly. Here in the ground near the edge of the grass was a boot print!

His fingers found it, and then felt carefully. It had been made by a running man, either large or heavily laden. Feeling his way along the tracks, London stopped again, for this time his hand had come in contact with a boot. He shook it, but there was no move or response. Crawling nearer he touched the man's hand. It was cold as marble in the damp night air.

Moving his hand again, he struck canvas. Feeling along it he found it was a long canvas sack. Evidently the dead man had grabbed this sack from the wagon and dashed for the shelter of the ditch or hollow. Apparently he had been struck by a bullet and killed, but, feeling again of the body, London's hand came in contact with a belt gun. So the Comanches had not found him! Stripping the belt and gun from the dead man, London swung it around his own hips, and then checked the gun. It was fully loaded, and so were the cartridge loops in the belt.

Something stirred in the grass, and instantly he froze, sliding out his hunting knife. He waited for several minutes, and then he heard it again. Something alive lay here in the grass with him!

A Comanche? No Indian likes to fight at night, and he had seen no Indians anywhere near when darkness fell. No, if anything lived near him now, it must be something, man or animal, from the wagon train. For a long time he lay still, thinking it over, and then he took a chance. Yet from his experience the chance was not a long one.

"If there is someone there, speak up."

There was no sound, and he waited, listening. Five minutes passed — ten — twenty. Carefully, then, he slid through the grass, changing his position, and then froze in place. Something was moving, quite near!

His hand shot out, and he was shocked to find himself grasping a small hand with a ruffle of cloth at the wrist! The child struggled violently, and he whispered hoarsely: "Be still. I'm a friend. If you run,

15

the Indians might come." Instantly the struggling stopped. "There," he breathed. "That's better." He searched his mind for something reassuring to say, and finally said: "Damp here, isn't it? Don't you have a coat?"

There was a momentary silence, and then a small voice said: "It was in the wagon."

"We'll look for it pretty soon," London said. "My name's Jim. What's yours?"

"Betty Jane Jones. I'm five years old and my papa's name is Daniel Jones and he is forty-six. Are you forty-six?"

London grinned. "No, I'm just twenty-nine, Betty Jane." He hesitated a minute, and then said: "Betty Jane, you strike me as a mighty brave little girl. There when I first heard you, you made no more noise than a rabbit. Now do you think you can keep that up?"

"Yes." It was a very small voice but it sounded sure.

"Good. Now listen, Betty Jane." Quietly he told her where he had come from and where he was going. He did not mention her parents, and she did not ask about them. From that he decided she knew only too well what had happened to them and the others from the wagon train.

"There's a canvas sack here, and I've got to look into it. Maybe there's something we can use. We're going to need food, Betty Jane, and a rifle. Later, we're going to have to find horses and money."

The sound of his voice, low though it was, seemed to give her confidence. She crawled nearer to him, and,

16

when she felt the sack, she said: "That's Daddy's bag. He keeps his carbine in it and his best clothes."

"Carbine?" London fumbled open the sack.

"Is a carbine like a rifle?"

He told her it was, and then found the gun. It was carefully wrapped, and by the feel of it London could tell the weapon was new or almost new. There was ammunition, another pistol, and a small canvas sack that chinked softly with gold coins. He stuffed this in his pocket. A careful check of the remaining wagons netted him nothing more, but he was not disturbed. The guns he had were good ones, and he had a little food and the canteen. Gravely he took Betty Jane's hand and they started.

They walked for an hour before her steps began to drag, and then he picked her up and carried her. By the time the sky had grown gray, he figured they had come six or seven miles from the burned wagons. He found some solid ground among some reeds on the edge of a slough, and they settled down there for the day.

After making coffee with a handful found in one of the only partly burned wagons, London gave Betty Jane some of the jerky and a biscuit. Then for the first time he examined his carbine. His eyes brightened as he sized it up. It was a Ball & Lamson Repeating Carbine, a gun just on the market and of which this must have been one of the first sold. It was a seven-shot weapon carrying a .56–50 cartridge. It was almost thirty-eight inches in length and weighed a bit over seven pounds.

The pistols were also new, both Prescott Navy six-shooters, caliber .38 with rosewood grips. Betty Jane looked at them and tears welled into her eyes. He took her hand quickly.

"Don't cry, honey. Your dad would want me to use the guns to take care of his girl. You've been mighty brave. Now keep it up."

She looked up at him with woebegone eyes, but the tears stopped, and after a while she fell asleep.

There was little shade, and, as the reeds were not tall, he did not dare stand up. They kept close to the edge of the reeds and lay perfectly still. Once he heard a horse walking not far away and heard low, guttural voices and a hacking cough. He caught only a fleeting glimpse of one rider and hoped the Indians would not find their tracks.

When night came, they started on once more. He took his direction by the stars and he walked steadily, carrying Betty Jane most of the distance. Sometimes when she walked beside him, she talked. She rambled on endlessly about her home, her dolls, and her parents. Then on the third day she mentioned Hurlburt.

"He was a bad man. My papa told Mama he was a bad man. Papa said he was after Mister Ballard's money."

"Who was Hurlburt?" London asked, more to keep the child occupied than because he wanted to know.

"He tried to steal Daddy's new carbine, and Mister Ballard said he was a thief. He told him so."

Hurlburt. The child might be mispronouncing the name, but it sounded like that. There had been a man

in Independence by that name. He had not been liked
— a big, bearded man, very quarrelsome.

"Did he have a beard, Betty Jane? A big, black
beard?"

She nodded eagerly. "At first, he did. But he didn't
have it when he came back with the Indians."

"What?" He turned so sharply toward her that her
eyes widened. He put his hand on her shoulder. "Did
you say this Hurlburt came back with the Indians?"

Seriously she nodded. "I saw him. He was in back of
them, but I saw him. He was the one who shot his gun
at Mister Ballard."

"You say he came back?" London asked. "You mean
he went away from the wagons before the attack?"

She looked at him. "Oh, yes! He went away when we
stopped by the big pool. Mister Ballard and Daddy
caught him taking things again. They put ropes on him,
on his hands and his feet. But when morning came, I
went to see, and he was gone away. Daddy said he had
left the wagons, and he hoped nothing would happen to
him."

Hurlburt. He had gone away and then had come
back with the Indians. A renegade, then. What had they
said of him in Independence? He had been over the
trail several times. Maybe he was working with the
Indians.

Betty Jane went to sleep on the grass he had pulled
for her to lie on, and Jim London made a careful
reconnaissance of the area, and then returned and lay
down himself. After a long time he dozed, dreaming of
Jane. He awakened feeling discouraged, with the last of

their food gone. He had not tried the rifle, although twice they had seen antelope. There was too much chance of being heard by Indians.

Betty Jane was noticeably thinner, and her face looked wan as she slept. Suddenly he heard a sound and looked up, almost too late. Not a dozen feet away a Comanche looked over the reeds and aimed a rifle at him! Hurling himself to one side, he jerked out one of the Navy pistols. The Comanche's rifle bellowed, and then Jim fired. The Indian threw up his rifle and fell over backward and lay still.

Carefully London looked around. The rim of the hills was unbroken, and there was no other Indian in sight. The Indian's spotted pony cropped grass not far away. Gun in hand, London walked to the Indian. The bullet from the pistol had struck him under the chin and, tearing out the back, had broken the man's neck. A scarcely dry scalp was affixed to his rawhide belt, and the rifle he carried was new.

He walked toward the horse. The animal shied back. "Take it easy, boy," London said softly. "You're all right." Surprisingly the horse perked up both ears and stared at him.

"Understand English, do you?" he said softly. "Well, maybe you're a white man's horse. We'll see."

He caught the reins and held out a hand to the horse. It hesitated, and then snuffed of his fingers. He moved up the reins to it and touched a palm to the animal's back. The bridle was a white man's, too. There was no saddle, however, only a blanket.

20

Betty Jane was crying softly when he reached her, obviously frightened by the guns. He picked her up, and then the rifle, and started back toward the horse. "Don't cry, honey. We've got a horse now."

She slept in his arms that night, and he did not stop riding. He rode all through the night until the little horse began to stumble, and then he dismounted and led the horse while Betty Jane rode. Just before daylight they rested.

Two days later, tired, unshaven, and bedraggled, Jim London rode down the dusty street of Cimarron toward the Maxwell House. It was bright in the afternoon sunlight, and the sun glistened on the flanks and shoulders of the saddled horses at the hitch rail. Drawing up before the house, London slid from the saddle. Maxwell was standing on the wide porch, staring down at him, and beside him was Tom Boggs, who London remembered from Missouri as the grandson of Daniel Boone.

"You look plumb tuckered, stranger, and that looks like an Injun rig on the horse. Or part of it."

"It is. The Indian's dead." He looked at Maxwell. "Is there a woman around here? This kid's nigh dead for rest and comfort."

"Sure!" Maxwell exclaimed heartily. "Lots of women around. My wife's inside." He took the sleeping child and called to his wife. As he did so, the child's eyes opened and stared, and then the corners of her mouth drew down and she screamed. All three men turned to where she looked. Hurlburt was standing there, gaping at the child as if the earth had opened before him.

"What is it?" Maxwell looked perplexed. "What's the matter?"

"That's the man who killed Mister Ballard! I saw him!"

Hurlburt's face paled. "*Aw*, the kid's mistook me for somebody else," he scoffed. "I never seen her before." He turned to Jim London. "Where'd you find that youngster?" he demanded. "Who are you?"

Jim London did not immediately reply. He was facing Hurlburt and suddenly all his anger and irritation at the trail, the Indians, the awful butchery around the wagons returned to him and boiled down to this man. A child without parents because of this man.

"I picked that child up on the ground near a burned-out, Indian-raided wagon train," he said. "The same train you left Missouri with."

Hurlburt's face darkened with angry blood.

"You lie," he declared viciously. "You lie!"

Jim did not draw. He stared at Hurlburt, his eyes unwavering. "How'd you get here, then? You were in Independence when I left there. No wagons passed us. You had to be with that Ballard train."

"I ain't been in Independence for two years," Hurlburt blustered. "You're crazy and so's that blasted kid."

"Seems kind of funny," Maxwell suggested, his eyes cold. "You sold two rifles after you got here, and you had gold money. There's a train due in, the boys tell

22

me. Maybe we better hold you until we ask them if you were in Independence."

"Like hell!" Hurlburt said furiously. "I ain't no renegade, and nobody holds me in no jail!"

Jim London took an easy step forward. "These guns I'm wearing, Hurlburt, belonged to Jones. I reckon he'd be glad to see this done. You led those Indians against those wagons. They found out you were a thief and faced you with it. I got it from Betty Jane, and the kid wouldn't lie about a thing like that. She told me all about it before we got here. So you don't get to go to jail. You don't get to wait. You get a chance to reach for a gun, and that's all."

Hurlburt's face was ugly. Desperately he glanced right and left. A crowd had gathered, but nobody spoke for him. He was up against it and he knew it. Suddenly he grabbed for his guns. Jim London's Prescott Navies leaped from their holsters, and the right one barked, a hard sharp report. Hurlburt backed up two steps, and then fell face down, a blue hole over his eye.

"Good work," Boggs said grimly. "I've had my doubts about that *hombre*. He never does nothing, but he always has money."

"Staying around?" Maxwell asked, looking at London.

"No," Jim said quietly. "My wife's waiting for me. I ain't seen her since 'Sixty-One."

"Since 'Sixty-One?" Boggs was incredulous. "You heard from her?"

"She didn't know where I was. Anyway, she never learned to write none." He flushed slightly. "I can't, neither. Only my name."

Lucian Maxwell looked away, clearing his throat. Then he said very carefully: "Better not rush any, son. That's a long time. It'll soon be five years."

"She'll be waiting." He looked at them, one to the other. "It was the war. They took me in the Army, and I fought all through."

"What about the kid?" Boggs asked.

"Come morning she'll be ready, I reckon. I'll take her with me. She'll need a home, and I sort of owe her something for this here rifle and the guns. Also" — he looked at them calmly — "I got nine hundred dollars in gold and bills here in my pocket. It's hers. I found it in her daddy's duffel." He cleared his throat. "I reckon that'll buy her a piece of any place we got and give her a home with us for life. We wanted a little girl, and while my wife . . . she was expecting . . . I don't know if anything come of it."

Both men were silent, and finally Maxwell said: "See here, London, your wife may be dead. She may have married again. Anyway, she couldn't have stayed on that ranch alone. Man, you'd better leave the child here with us. Take the money. You earned it, packing her here, but let her stay until you find out."

London shook his head patiently. "You don't understand," he said, "that's my Jane who's waiting. She told me she'd wait for me, and she don't say things light. Not her."

"Where is she?" Maxwell asked curiously.

"We got us a place up on North Fork. Good grass, water, and timber. The wife likes trees. I built us a cabin there, and a lean-to. We aimed to put about forty acres to wheat and maybe set us up a mill." He looked up at them, smiling a little. "Pa was a miller, and he always said to me that folks need bread wherever they are. 'Make a good loaf,' he said, 'and you'll always have a good living.' He had him a mill up Oregon way."

"North Fork?" Boggs and Maxwell exchanged glances. "Man, that country was run over by Injuns two years ago. Some folks went back up there, but one o' them is Bill Ketchum. He's got a bunch running with him no bettern'n he is. Hoss thieves, folks reckon. Most anything to get the 'coon."

When he rounded the bend below the creek and saw the old bridge ahead of him, his mouth got dry and his heart began to pound. He walked his horse, with the child sitting before him and the carbine in its scabbard. At the creek he drew up for just a moment, looking down at the bridge. He had built it with his own hands. Then his eyes saw the hand rail on the right. It was cut from a young poplar. He had used cedar. Somebody had worked on that bridge recently.

The cabin he had built topped a low rise in a clearing backed by a rocky overhang. He rode through the pines, trying to quiet himself. It might be like they said. Maybe she had sold out and gone away, or just gone. Maybe she had married somebody else, or maybe the Indians . . .

The voice he heard was coarse and amused. "Come off it!" the voice said. "From here on you're my woman. I ain't takin' no more of this guff!"

25

Jim London did not stop his horse when it entered the clearing. He let it walk right along, but he lifted the child from in front of him and said: "Betty Jane, that lady over yonder is your new ma. You run to her now, an' tell her your name is Jane. Hear me?"

He lowered the child to the ground and she scampered at once toward the slender woman with the wide gray eyes who stood on the step staring at the rider.

Bill Ketchum turned abruptly to see what her expression meant. The lean, raw-boned man on the horse had a narrow sun-browned face and a battered hat pulled low. The rider shoved it back now and rested his right hand on his thigh. Ketchum stared at him. Something in that steel-trap jaw and those hard eyes sent a chill through him.

"I take it," London said gravely, "that you are Bill Ketchum. I heard what you said just now. I also heard down the line that you were a horse thief, maybe worse. You get off this place now, and don't ever come back. You do and I'll shoot you on sight. Now get!"

"You talk mighty big." Ketchum stared at him, anger rising within him. Should he try this fellow? Who did he think he was, anyway?

"I'm big as I talk," London said flatly. "I done killed a man yesterday down to Maxwell's. *Hombre* name of Hurlburt. That's all I figure to kill this week unless you want to make it two. Start moving now."

Ketchum hesitated, then viciously reined his horse around and started down the trail. As he neared the edge of the woods, rage suddenly possessed him. He

26

grabbed for his rifle and instantly a shot rang out and a heavy slug gouged the butt of his rifle and glanced off.

Beyond him the words were plain. "I put that one right where I wanted it. This here's a seven-shot repeater, so if you want one through your heart, just try it again."

London waited until the man had disappeared in the trees, and a minute more. Only then did he turn to his wife. She was down on the step with her arm around Betty Jane, who was sobbing happily against her breast.

"Jim," she whispered. "Oh, Jim."

He got down heavily. He started toward her, and then stopped. Around the corner came a boy of four or five, a husky youngster with a stick in his hand and his eyes blazing. When he saw Jim, he stopped abruptly. This stranger looked just like the old picture on his mother's table. Only he had on a coat in the picture, a store-bought coat.

"Jim." Jane was on her feet now, color coming back into her face. "This is Little Jim. This is your son."

Jim London swallowed and his throat suddenly filled. He looked at his wife and started toward her. He felt awkward, clumsy. He took her by the elbows. "Been a long time, honey," he said hoarsely, "a mighty long time."

She drew back a little nervously. "Let's . . . I've coffee on. We'll . . ." She turned and hurried toward the door, and he followed.

It would take some time. A little time for both of them to get over feeling strange, and maybe more time for her. She was a woman, and women needed time to get used to things.

He turned his head and almost automatically his eyes went to that south forty. The field was green with a young crop. Wheat! He smiled.

She had filled his cup; he dropped into a seat, and she sat down opposite him. Little Jim looked awkwardly at Betty Jane, and she stared at him with round, curious eyes.

"There's a big frog down by the bridge," Little Jim said suddenly. "I bet I can make him hop."

They ran outside into the sunlight, and across the table Jim London took his wife's hand. It was good to be home. Mighty good.

Fork Your Own Broncs

Mac Marcy turned in the saddle and, resting his left hand on the cantle, glanced back up the arroyo. His lean, brown face was troubled. There were cattle here, all right, but too few.

At this time of day, late afternoon and very hot, there should have been a steady drift of cattle toward the water hole.

Ahead of him he heard a steer bawl and then another. Now what? Above the bawling of the cattle he heard another sound, a sound that turned his face gray with worry. It was the sound of hammers.

He needed nothing more to tell him what was happening. Jingle Bob Kenyon was fencing the water hole!

As he rounded the bend in the wash, the sound of hammers ceased for an instant, but only for an instant. Then they continued with their work.

Two strands of barbed wire had already been stretched tight and hard across the mouth of the wash. Several cowhands were stretching the third wire of what was obviously to be a four-wire fence.

Already Marcy's cattle were bunching near the fence, bawling for water.

As he rode nearer, two men dropped their hammers and lounged up to the fence. Marcy's eyes narrowed

29

and his gaze shifted to the big man on the roan horse. Jingle Bob Kenyon was watching him with grim humor.

Marcy avoided the eyes of the two other men by the fence, Vin Ricker and John Soley, who could mean only one thing for him — trouble, bad trouble. Vin Ricker was a gun hand and a killer. John Soley was anything Vin told him to be.

"This is a rotten trick, Kenyon," Marcy declared angrily. "In this heat my herd will be wiped out."

Kenyon's eyes were unrelenting. "That's just tough," he stated flatly. "I warned you when you fust come in here to git out while the gittin' was good. You stayed on. You asked for it. Now you take it or git out."

Temper flaring within him like a burst of flame, Marcy glared. But deliberately he throttled his fury. He would have no chance here. Ricker and Soley were too much for him, let alone the other hands and Kenyon himself.

"If you don't like it," Ricker sneered, "why don't you stop us? I hear tell you're a plumb salty *hombre*."

"You'd like me to give you a chance to kill me, wouldn't you?" Marcy asked harshly. "Someday I'll get you without your guns, Ricker, and I'll tear down your meat house."

Ricker laughed. "I don't want to dirty my hands on you, or I'd come over an' make you eat those words. If you ever catch me without these guns, you'll wish to old Harry I still had 'em."

Marcy turned his eyes away from the gunman and looked at Kenyon.

30

"Kenyon, I didn't think this of you. Without water, my cows won't last three days, and you know it. You'll bust me flat."

Kenyon was unrelenting. "This is a man's country, Marcy," he said dryly. "You fork your own bronc's an' you git your own water. Don't come whinin' to me. You moved in on me, an', if you git along, it'll be on your own."

Kenyon turned his horse and rode away. For an instant Marcy stared after him, seething with rage. Then, abruptly, he wheeled his grayish-black horse — a moros — and started back up the arroyo. Even as he turned, he became aware that only six lean steers faced the barbed wire.

He had ridden but a few yards beyond the bend when that thought struck him like a blow. Six head of all the hundreds he had herded in here. By rights they should all be at the water hole or heading that way. Puzzled, he started back up the trail.

By rights, there should be a big herd here. Where could the cattle be? As he rode back toward his claim shack, he stared about him. No cattle were in sight. His range was stripped.

Rustlers? He scowled. But there had been no rustling activity of which he had heard. Ricker and Soley were certainly the type to rustle cattle, but Marcy knew Kenyon had been keeping them busy on the home range.

He rode back toward the shack, his heart heavy.

He had saved for seven years, riding cattle trails to Dodge, Abilene, and Ellsworth to get the money to buy his herd. It was his big chance to have a spread of his own, a chance for some independence and a home.

A home. He stared bitterly at the looming rimrock behind his outfit. A home meant a wife, and there was only one girl in the world for him. There would never be another who could make him feel as Sally Kenyon did. But she would have to be old Jingle Bob's daughter.

Not that she had ever noticed him. But in those first months before the fight with Jingle Bob became dog-eat-dog, Marcy had seen her around, watched her, been in love with her from a distance. He had always hoped that when his place had proved up and he was settled, he might know her better. He might even ask her to marry him.

It had been a foolish dream. Yet day by day it became even more absurd. He was not only in a fight with her father, but he was closer than ever to being broke.

Grimly, his mind fraught with worry, he cooked his meager supper, crouching before the fireplace. Again and again the thought kept recurring — where were his cattle? If they had been stolen, they would have to be taken down past the water hole and across Jingle Bob's range. There was no other route from Marcy's corner of range against the rim. For a horseman, yes. But not for cattle.

The sound of a walking horse startled him. He straightened, and then stepped away from the fire and put the bacon upon the plate, listening to the horse as it drew nearer. Then he put down his food, and, loosening his gun, he stepped to the door.

The sun had set long since, but it was not yet dark. He watched a gray horse coming down from the trees leading up to the rim. Suddenly he gulped in surprise.

It was Sally Kenyon! He stepped outside and walked into the open. The girl saw him and waved a casual hand, and then reined in.

"Have you a drink of water?" she asked, smiling. "It's hot, riding."

"Sure," he said, trying to smile. "Coffee, if you want. I was just fixing to eat a mite. Want to join me? Of course," he said sheepishly, "I ain't no hand with grub."

"I might take some coffee."

Sally swung down, drawing off her gauntlets. She had always seemed a tall girl, but on the ground she came just to his shoulder. Her hair was honey-colored, her eyes gray.

He caught the quick glance of her eyes as she looked around. He saw them hesitate with surprise at the spectacle of flowers blooming near the door. She looked up, and their eyes met.

"Ain't much time to work around," he confessed. "I've sort of been trying to make it look like a home."

"Did you plant the flowers?" she asked curiously.

"Yes, ma'am. My mother was always a great hand for flowers. I like 'em, too, so when I built this cabin, I set some out. The wildflowers, I transplanted."

He poured coffee into a cup and handed it to her. She sipped the hot liquid and looked at him.

"I've been hearing about you," she said.

"From Jingle Bob?"

She nodded. "And some others. Vin Ricker, for one. He hates you."

"Who else?"

"Chen Lee."

"Lee?" Marcy shook his head. "I don't place him."

"He's Chinese, our cook. He seems to know a great deal about you. He thinks you're a fine man. A great fighter, too. He's always talking about some Mullen gang you had trouble with."

"Mullen gang?" He stared. "Why, that was in . . ." He caught himself. "No, ma'am, I reckon he's mistook. I don't know any Chinese and there ain't no Mullen gang around I know of."

That, he reflected, was no falsehood. The Mullen gang had all fitted very neatly into the boothill he had prepared for them back in Bentown. They definitely weren't around.

"Going to stay here?" she asked, looking at him over her coffee cup, her gray eyes level.

His eyes flashed. "I was fixing to, but I reckon your old man has stopped me by fencing that water hole. He's a hard man, your father."

"It's a hard country." She did not smile. "He's got ideas about it. He drove the Mescaleros out. He wiped out the rustlers. He took this range. He doesn't like the idea of any soft-going, second-run cowhand coming in and taking over."

His head jerked up.

"Soft-going?" he flared. "Second-run? Why, that old billy goat."

Sally turned toward her horse. "Don't tell me. Tell him. If you've nerve enough."

He got up and took the bridle of her horse. His eyes were hard.

"Ma'am," he said, striving to make his voice gentle, "I think you're a mighty fine person, and sure enough pretty, but that father of yours is a rough-riding old buzzard. If it wasn't for that Ricker *hombre* . . ."

"Afraid?" she taunted, looking down at him.

"No, ma'am," he said quietly. "Only I ain't a killing man. I was raised a Quaker. I don't aim to do no fighting."

"You're in a fighting man's country," she warned him. "And you are cutting in on a fighting man's range."

She turned her gray and started to ride away. Suddenly she reined in and looked back over her shoulder.

"By the way," she said, "there's water up on the rim."

Water up on the rim? What did she mean? He turned his head and stared up at the top of the great cliff, which loomed high overhead into the night. It was fully a mile away, but it seemed almost behind his house.

How could he get up to the rim? Sally had come from that direction. In the morning he would try. In the distance, carried by the still air of night, he heard a cow bawling. It was shut off from the water hole. His six head, starving for water.

Marcy walked out to the corral and threw a saddle on the moros. He swung into the saddle and rode at a canter toward the water hole.

They heard him coming, and he saw a movement in the shadows by the cottonwoods.

"Hold it!" a voice called. "What do you want?"

"Let that fence down and put them cows through!" Marcy yelled.

There was a harsh laugh. "Sorry, *amigo*. No can do. Only Kenyon cows drink here."

"All right," Marcy snapped. "They are Kenyon cows. I'm giving 'em to him. Let the fence down and let 'em drink. I ain't seeing no animal die just to please an old plug head. Let 'em through."

Then he heard Sally's voice. He saw her sitting her horse beside old Joe Linger, who was her bodyguard, teacher, and friend. An old man who had taught her to ride and to shoot and who had been a scout for the Army at some time in the past.

Sally was speaking, and he heard her say: "Let them through, Texas. If they are our cows, we don't want to have them die on us."

Marcy turned the moros and rode back toward his cabin, a sense of defeat heavy upon him . . .

He rolled out of his blankets with the sun and, after a quick breakfast, saddled the grayish-black horse and started back toward the rim. He kept remembering Sally's words. There is water on the rim. Why had she told him that? What good would water do him if it was way up on the rim?

There must be a way up. By backtracking the girl, he could find it. He was worried about the cattle. The problem of their disappearance kept working into his thoughts. That was another reason for his ride, the major reason. If the cattle were still on his ranch, they were back in the breaks at the foot of the rim.

As he backtracked the girl's horse, he saw cow tracks, more and more of them. Obviously some of his cattle had drifted this way. It puzzled him, yet he had to admit that he knew little of this country.

Scarcely a year before he had come into this range, and, when he arrived, the grass in the lower reaches of the valley was good, and there were mesquite beans. The cattle grew fat. With hotter and dryer weather, they had shown more and more of a tendency to keep to shady hillsides and to the cañons.

The cow tracks scattered out and disappeared. He continued on the girl's trail. He was growing more and more puzzled, for he was in the shadow of the great cliff now, and any trail that mounted it must be frightfully steep. Sally, of course, had grown up in this country on horseback. With her always had been Joe Linger. Old Joe had been one of the first white men to settle in the rim country.

Marcy skirted a clump of piñon and emerged on a little sandy level at the foot of the cliff. This, at one distant time, had been a streambed, a steep stream that originated somewhere back up in the rimrock and flowed down here and deeper into his range.

Then he saw the trail. It was a narrow catwalk of rock that clung to the cliffs edge in a way that made him swallow as he looked at it. The catwalk led up the face of the cliff and back into a deep gash in the face of the rim, a gash invisible from below.

The moros snorted a few times, but true to its mountain blood it took the trail on dainty feet. In an hour Marcy rode out on the rim itself. All was green here, green grass. The foliage on the trees was greener than below. There was every indication of water, but no sign of a cow. Not even a range-bred cow would go up such a trail as Marcy had just ridden.

Following the tracks of the gray, Marcy worked back through the cedar and piñon until he began to hear a muffled roar. Then he rode through the trees and reined in at the edge of a pool that was some twenty feet across. Water flowed into it from a fair-size stream, bubbling over rocks and falling into the pool. There were a number of springs here, and undoubtedly the supply of water was limitless. But where did it go?

Dismounting, Marcy walked down to the edge of the water and knelt on a flat rock and leaned far out.

Brush hung far out over the water at the end of the pool, brush that grew on a rocky ledge no more than three feet above the surface of the water. But beneath that ledge was a black hole at least eight feet long. Water from the pool was pouring into that black hole.

Mac Marcy got up and walked around the pool to the ledge. The brush was very thick, and he had to force his way through. Clinging precariously to a clump of manzanita, he leaned out over the rim of the ledge and tried to peer into the hole. He could see nothing except a black slope of water and that the water fell steeply beyond that slope.

He leaned farther out, felt the manzanita give way slowly, and made a wild clutch at the neighboring brush. Then he plunged into the icy waters of the pool.

He felt himself going down, down, down! He struck out, trying to swim, but the current caught him and swept him into the gaping mouth of the wide black hole under the ledge.

Darkness closed over his head. He felt himself shooting downward. He struck something and felt it give beneath him, and then something hit him a powerful blow on the head. Blackness and icy water closed over him.

Chattering teeth awakened him. He was chilled to the bone and soaking wet. For a moment he lay on hard, smooth rock in darkness, head throbbing, trying to realize what had happened. His feet felt cold. He pulled them up and turned over to a sitting position in a large cave. Only then did he realize his feet had been lying in a pool of water.

Far above he could see a faint glimmer of light, a glimmer feebly reflecting from the black, glistening roar of a fall. He tilted his head back and stared upward through the gloom. That dim light, the hole through which he had come, was at least sixty feet above him!

In falling he had struck some obstruction in the narrow chimney of the water's course, some piece of driftwood or brush insecurely wedged across the hole. It had broken his descent and had saved him.

His matches would be useless. Feeling around the cave floor in the dark, he found some dry tinder that had been lying here for years. He still had his guns, since they had been tied in place with rawhide thongs. He drew one of them, extracted a cartridge, and went to work on it with his hunting knife.

When it was open, he placed it carefully on the rock beside him. Then he cut shavings and crushed dried bark in his hand. Atop this he placed the powder from the open cartridge.

Then he went to work to strike a spark from a rock with the steel back of his knife. There was not the slightest wind here. Despite that, he worked for the better part of an hour before a spark sprang into the powder.

There was a bright burst of flame and the shavings crackled. He added fuel and then straightened up and stepped back to look around.

He stood on a wide ledge in the gloomy, closed cavern at the foot of the fall's first drop, down which he had fallen. The water struck the rock not ten feet away from him. Then it took another steep drop off to the left. He could see by the driftwood that had fallen clear that it was the usual thing for the rushing water to cast all water-borne objects onto this ledge.

The ledge had at one time been deeply gouged and worn by running water. Picking up a torch, Marcy turned and glanced away into the darkness. There lay the old dry channel, deeply worn and polished by former running water.

At some time in the past, this had been the route of the stream underground. In an earthquake or some breakthrough of the rock, the water had taken the new course.

Thoughtfully Marcy calculated his situation. He was fearful of his predicament. From the first moment of consciousness in that utter darkness, he had been so. There is no fear more universal than the fear of entombment alive, the fear of choking, strangling in utter darkness beyond the reach of help.

Mac Marcy was no fool. He was, he knew, beyond the reach of help. The moros was ground-hitched in a spot where there was plenty of grass and water. The grayish-black horse would stay right there.

No one, with the exception of Sally, ever went to the top of the rim. It was highly improbable that she would go again soon. In many cases, weeks would go by without anyone stopping by Marcy's lonely cabin. If he was going to get out of this hole, he would have to do it by his own efforts.

One glance up that fall showed him there was no chance of going back up the way he had come down. Working his way over to the next step downward of the fall, he held out his torch and peered below. All was utter blackness, with only the cold damp of falling water in the air.

Fear was mounting within him now, but he fought it back, forcing himself to be calm and to think carefully. The old dry channel remained a vague hope. But to all appearances it went deeper and deeper into the Stygian blackness of the earth. He put more fuel on his fire and started exploring again. Fortunately the wood he was burning was bone dry and made almost no smoke.

Torch in hand he started down the old dry channel. This had been a watercourse for many, many years. The rock was worn and polished. He had gone no more than sixty feet when the channel divided.

On the left was a black, forbidding hole, scarcely waist high. Down that route most of the water seemed to have gone, as it was worn the deepest.

On the right was an opening almost like a doorway. Marcy stepped over to it and held his torch out. It also was a black hole. He had a sensation of awful depth. Stepping back, he picked up a rock. Leaning out, he dropped it into the hole on the right.

For a long time he listened. Then, somewhere far below, there was a splash. This hole was literally hundreds of feet deep. It would end far below the level of the land on which his cabin stood.

He drew back. Sweat stood out on his forehead, and, when he put his hand to it, his brow felt cold and clammy. He looked at the black waist-high hole on the left and felt fear rise within him as he had never felt it before. He drew back and wet his lips.

His torch was almost burned out. Turning with the last of its light, he retraced his steps to the ledge by the fall.

How long he had been below ground, he didn't know. He looked up, and there was still a feeble light from above. But it seemed to have grown less. Had night almost come?

Slowly he built a new torch. This was his last chance of escape. It was a chance he had already begun to give

42

up. Of them all, that black hole on the left was least promising, but he must explore it.

He pulled his hat down a little tighter and started back to where the tunnel divided into two holes. His jaw was set grimly. He got down on his hands and knees and edged into the black hole on the left.

Once inside, he found it fell away steeply in a mass of loose boulders. Scrambling over them, he came to a straight, steep fall of at least ten feet. Glancing at the sheer drop, he knew one thing — once down there, he would never get back up.

Holding his torch high, he looked beyond. Nothing but darkness. Behind him there was no hope. He hesitated, and then got down on his hands and knees, lowered himself over the edge, and dropped ten feet.

This time he had to be right, for there was no going back. He walked down a slanting tunnel. It seemed to be growing darker. Glancing up at his torch, he saw it was burning out. In a matter of minutes he would be in total darkness.

He walked faster and faster. Then he broke into a stumbling run, fear rising within him. Something brought him up short, and for a moment he did not see what had caused him to halt in his blind rush. Then hope broke over him like a cold shower of rain.

There on the sand beneath his feet were tiny tracks. He bent over them. A pack rat or some other tiny creature. Getting up, he hurried on, and, seeing a faint glow ahead, he rushed around a bend. There before him was the feeble glow of the fading day. His torch guttered and went out.

He walked on to the cave mouth, trembling in every limb. Mac Marcy was standing in an old watercourse that came out from behind some boulders not two miles from his cabin. He stumbled home and fell into his bunk, almost too tired to undress.

Marcy awakened to a frantic pounding on his door. Staggering erect, he pulled on his boots, yelling out as he did so. Then he drew on his Levi's and shirt and opened the door, buttoning his shirt with one hand.

Sally, her face deathly pale, was standing outside. Beyond her gray mare stood Marcy's moros. At the sight of him the grayish-black horse lifted his head and pricked up his ears.

"Oh," Sally gasped. "I thought you were dead . . . drowned."

He stepped over beside her.

"No," he said, "I guess I'm still here. You're pretty scared, ma'am. What's there for you to be scared about?"

"Why," she burst out impatiently, "if you . . ." She caught herself and stopped abruptly. "After all," she continued coolly, "no one wants to find a friend drowned."

"Ma'am," he said sincerely, "if you get that wrought up, I'll get myself almost drowned every day."

She stared at him and then smiled. "I think you're a fool," she said. She mounted and turned. "But a nice fool."

Marcy stared after her thoughtfully. Well now, maybe . . .

He glanced down at his boots. Where they had lain in the pool, there was water stain on them. Also, there was a small green leaf clinging to the rough leather. He stooped and picked it off, wadded it up, and started to throw it away when he was struck by an idea. He unfolded the leaf and studied the veins. Suddenly his face broke into a grin.

"Boy," he said to the moros, "we got us a job to do, even if you do need a rest." He swung into the saddle and rode back toward the watercourse, still grinning.

It was mid-afternoon when he returned to the cabin and ate a leisurely lunch, still chuckling. Then he mounted again and started for the old water hole that had been fenced by Jingle Bob Kenyon.

When Marcy rounded the bend, he could see that something was wrong. A dozen men were gathered around the water hole. Nearby and astride her gray was Sally.

The men were in serious conference, and they did not notice Marcy's approach. He rode up, leaning on the horn of the saddle, and watched them, smiling.

Suddenly Vin Ricker looked up. His face went hard. Mac Marcy swung down and strolled up to the fence, leaning casually on a post.

"What's up?"

"The water hole's gone dry!" Kenyon exploded. "Not a drop o' water in it."

Smothering a grin, Marcy rolled a smoke.

"Well," he said philosophically, "the Lord giveth and He taketh away. No doubt it's the curse of the Lord for your greed, Jingle Bob."

Kenyon glared at him suspiciously. "You know somethin' about this?" he demanded. "Man, in this hot weather my cattle will die by the hundreds. Somethin's got to be done."

"Seems to me," Marcy said dryly, "I have heard those words before."

Sally was looking at him over her father's head, her face grave and questioning. But she said nothing, gave no sign of approval or disapproval.

"This here's a man's country," Marcy said seriously. "You fork your own bronc's and you get your own water."

Kenyon flushed. "Marcy, if you know anythin' about this, for goodness sake spill it. My cows will die. Maybe I was too stiff about this, but there's somethin' mighty funny goin' on here. This water hole ain't failed in twenty years."

"Let me handle him," Ricker snarled. "I'm just achin' to git my hands on him."

"Don't ache too hard, or you'll git your wish," Marcy drawled, and he crawled through the fence. "All right, Kenyon, we'll talk business," Marcy said to the rancher. "You had me stuck yesterday with my tail in a crack. Now you got yours in one. I cut off your water to teach you a lesson. You're a blamed old highbinder, and it's high time you had some teeth pulled.

"Nobody but me knows how that water's cut off and where. If I don't change it, nobody can. So listen to what I'm saying. I'm going to have all the water I need after this on my own place, but this here hole stays open. No fences.

"This morning, when I went up to cut off your water, I saw some cow tracks. I'm missing a powerful lot of cows. I followed the tracks into a hidden draw and found three hundred of my cattle and about a hundred head of yours, all nicely corralled and ready to be herded across the border.

"While I was looking over the hide-out, I spied Ricker there. John Soley then came riding up with about thirty head of your cattle, and they run 'em in with the rest."

"You're a liar!" Ricker burst out, his face tense, and he dropped into a crouch, his fingers spread.

Marcy was unmoved. "No, I ain't bluffing. You try to prove where you were about nine this morning. And don't go trying to get me into a gunfight. I ain't a-going to draw, and you don't dare shoot me down in front of witnesses. But you take off those guns, and I'll . . ."

Ricker's face was ugly. "You bet I'll take 'em off! I allus did want a crack at that purty face o' yours."

He stripped off his guns and swung them to Soley in one movement. Then he rushed.

A wicked right swing caught Marcy before he dropped his gun belt and got his hands up, and it knocked him reeling into the dirt.

Ricker charged, his face livid, trying to kick Marcy with his boots, but Marcy rolled over and got on his feet. He lunged and swung a right that clipped Ricker on the temple. Then Marcy stabbed the rustler with a long left. They started to slug.

Neither had any knowledge of science. Both were raw and tough and hard-bitten. Toe to toe, bloody and bitter, they slugged it out. Ricker, confident and the larger of the two men, rushed in swinging. One of his swings cut Marcy's eye; another started blood gushing from Marcy's nose. Ricker set himself and threw a hard right for Marcy's chin, but the punch missed as Marcy swung one to the body that staggered Ricker.

They came in again, and Marcy's big fist pulped the rustler's lips, smashing him back on his heels. Then Marcy followed it in, swinging with both hands. His breath came in great gasps, but his eyes were blazing. He charged in, following Ricker relentlessly.

Suddenly Marcy's right caught the gunman and knocked him to his knees. Marcy stepped back and let him get up, and then knocked him sliding on his face in the sand. Ricker tried to get up, but he fell back, bloody and beaten.

Swiftly, before the slow-thinking Soley realized what was happening, Marcy spun and grabbed one of his own guns and turned it on this rustler.

"Drop 'em," he snapped. "Unbuckle your belt and step back."

Jingle Bob Kenyon leaned on his saddle horn, chewing his pipe stem thoughtfully.

"What," he drawled, "would you have done if he drawed his gun?"

Marcy looked up, surprised. "Why, I'd have killed him, of course." He glanced over at Sally, and then looked back at Kenyon. "Before we get off the subject," he said, "we finish our deal. I'll turn your water back into this hole . . . I got it stopped up away back inside the mountain . . . but, as I said, the hole stays open to anybody. Also" — Marcy's face colored a little — "I'm marrying Sally."

"You're what?" Kenyon glared, and then jerked around to look at his daughter.

Sally's eyes were bright. "You heard him, Father," she replied coolly. "I'm taking back with me those six steers he gave you so he can get them to water."

Marcy was looking at Kenyon when suddenly Marcy grinned.

"I reckon," he said, "you had your lesson. Sally and me have got a lot of talking to do."

Marcy swung aboard the moros, and he and Sally started off together.

Jingle Bob Kenyon stared after them, grim humor in his eyes.

"I wonder," he said, "what he would have done if Ricker had drawed?"

Old Joe Linger grinned and looked over at Kenyon from under his bushy brows. "Jest what he said. He'd've kilt him. That's Quaker John McMarcy, the *hombre* that wiped out the Mullen gang single-handed. He jest don't like to fight, that's all."

"It sure does beat all," Kenyon said thoughtfully. "The trouble a man has to go to git him a good son-in-law these days."

Riding for the Brand

He had been watching the covered wagon for more than an hour. There had been no movement, no sound. The bodies of the two animals that had drawn the wagon lay in the grass, plainly visible. Farther away, almost a mile away, stood a lone buffalo bull, black against the gray distance.

Nothing moved near the wagon, but Jed Asbury had lived too long in Indian country to risk his scalp on appearances, and he knew an Indian could lie ghost-still for hours on end. He had no intention of taking such a chance, stark naked and without weapons.

Two days before he had been stripped to the hide by Indians and forced to run the gauntlet, but he had run better than they had expected and had escaped with only a few minor wounds.

Now, miles away, he had reached the limit of his endurance. Despite little water and less food he was still in traveling condition except for his feet. They were lacerated and swollen, caked with dried blood.

Warily he started forward, taking advantage of every bit of cover and moving steadily toward the wagon. When he was within fifty feet, he settled down in the grass to study the situation.

This was the scene of an attack. Evidently the wagon had been alone, and the bodies of two men and a woman lay stretched on the grass. Clothing, papers, and cooking utensils were scattered, evidence of a hasty looting. Whatever had been the dreams of these people, they were ended now, another sacrifice to the westward march of empire. And the dead would not begrudge him what he needed.

Rising from the grass, he went cautiously to the wagon, a tall, powerfully muscled young man, unshaven and untrimmed.

He avoided the bodies. Oddly they were not mutilated, which was unusual, and the men still wore their boots. As a last resort he would take a pair for himself. First, he must examine the wagon.

If Indians had looted the wagon, they had done so hurriedly, for the interior of the wagon was in the wildest state of confusion. In the bottom of a trunk he found a fine black broadcloth suit as well as a new pair of hand-tooled leather boots, a woolen shirt, and several white shirts.

"Somebody's Sunday-go-to-meetin' outfit," he muttered. "Hadn't better try the boots on the way my feet are swollen."

He found clean underwear and dressed, putting on some rougher clothes that he found in the same chest. When he was dressed enough to protect him from the sun, he took water from a half empty barrel on the side of the wagon and bathed his feet; then he bandaged them with strips of white cloth torn from a dress.

His feet felt much better, and, as the boots were a size larger than he usually wore, he tried them. There was some discomfort, but he could wear them.

With a shovel tied to the wagon's side, he dug a grave and buried the three side-by-side, covered them with quilts from the wagon, filled in the earth, and piled stones over the grave. Then, hat in hand, he recited the Twenty-Third Psalm.

The savages or whoever had killed them had made only a hasty search, so now he went to the wagon to find whatever might be useful to him or might inform him as to the identity of the dead.

There were some legal papers, a will, and a handful of letters. Putting these to one side with a poncho he found, he spotted a sewing basket. Remembering his grandmother's habits, he emptied out the needles and thread, and under the padded bottom of the basket he found a large sealed envelope.

Ripping it open, he grunted with satisfaction. Wrapped in carefully folded tissue paper were twenty $20 gold pieces. Pocketing them, he delved deeper into the trunk. He found more carefully folded clothes. Several times he broke off his searching of the wagon to survey the country about, but saw nothing. The wagon was in a concealed situation where a rider might have passed within a few yards and not seen it. He seemed to have approached from the only angle from which it was visible.

In the very bottom of the trunk he struck pay dirt. He found a steel box. With a pick he forced it open. Inside, on folded velvet, lay a magnificent set of pistols,

52

silver-plated and beautifully engraved, with pearl handles. Wrapped in a towel nearby he found a pair of black leather cartridge belts and twin holsters. With them was a sack of .44 cartridges. Promptly he loaded the guns, and then stuffed the loops of both cartridge belts. After that, he tried the balance of the guns. The rest of the cartridges he dropped into his pockets.

In another fold of the cloth he found a pearl-handled knife of finely tempered steel, a Spanish fighting knife and a beautiful piece of work. He slung the scabbard around his neck with the haft just below his collar.

Getting his new possessions together, he made a pack of the clothing inside the poncho and used string to make a back pack of it. In the inside pocket of the coat he stowed the legal papers and the letters. In his hip pocket he stuffed a small leather-bound book he had found among the scattered contents of the wagon. He read little, but knew the value of a good book.

He had had three years of intermittent schooling, learning to read, write, and cipher a little.

There was a canteen and he filled it. Rummaging in the wagon he found the grub box almost empty, a little coffee, some moldy bread, and nothing else useful. He took the coffee, a small pot, and a tin cup. Then he glanced at the sun and started away.

Jed Asbury was accustomed to fending for himself. That there could be anything wrong in appropriating what he had found never entered his head, nor would it have entered the head of any other man at the time. Life was hard, and one lived as best one might. If the dead had any heirs, there would be a clue in the letters or the will. He would pay them when he could. No man would begrudge him taking what was needed to survive, but to repay the debt incurred was a foregone conclusion.

Jed had been born on an Ohio farm, his parents dying when he was ten years old. He had been sent to a crabbed uncle living in a Maine fishing village. For three years his uncle worked him like a slave, sending him out on the Banks with a fishing boat. Finally Jed had abandoned the boat, deep-sea fishing, and his uncle.

He had walked to Boston and by devious methods reached Philadelphia. He had run errands, worked in a mill, and then gotten a job as a printer's devil. He had grown to like a man who came often to the shop, a quiet man with dark hair and large gray eyes, his head curiously wide across the temples. The man wrote stories and literary criticism and occasionally loaned Jed books to read. His name was Edgar Poe and he was reported to be the foster son of John Allan, said to be the richest man in Virginia.

When Jed left the print shop, it was to ship on a windjammer for a voyage around the Horn. From San Francisco he had gone to Australia for a year in the gold fields, and then to South Africa and back to New York. He was twenty then and a big, well-made young man hardened by the life he had lived. He had gone on a riverboat down the Mississippi to Natchez and New Orleans.

In New Orleans, Jem Mace had taught him to box. Until then all he had known about fighting had been acquired through rough-and-tumble. From New Orleans he had gone to Havana, to Brazil, and then back to the States. In Natchez he had caught a cardsharp cheating. Jed Asbury had proved a bit quicker, and the gambler died, a victim of six-shooter justice. Jed left town just ahead of several of the gambler's irate companions.

On a Missouri River steamboat he had gone up to Fort Benton and then overland to Bannock. He had traveled with wagon freighters to Laramie, and then to Dodge.

In Tascosa he had encountered a brother of the dead Natchez gambler accompanied by two of the irate companions. He had killed two of his enemies and wounded the other, coming out of the fracas with a bullet in his leg. He traveled on to Santa Fe.

At twenty-four he was footloose and looking for a destination. Working as a bullwhacker he made a round trip to Council Bluffs, and then joined a wagon train for Cheyenne. The Comanches, raiding north, had interfered, and he had been the sole survivor.

He knew about where he was now, somewhere south and west of Dodge, but probably closer to Santa Fe than to the trail town. He should not be far from the cattle trail leading past Tascosa, so he headed that way. Along the river bottoms there should be strays lost from previous herds, so he could eat until a trail herd came along.

Walking a dusty trail in the heat, he shifted his small pack constantly and kept turning to scan the country over which he had come. He was in the heart of Indian country.

On the morning of the third day he sighted a trail herd, headed for Kansas. As he walked toward the herd, two of the three horsemen riding point turned toward him.

One was a lean, red-faced man with a yellowed mustache and a gleam of quizzical humor around his eyes. The other was a stocky, friendly rider on a paint horse.

"Howdy!" The older man's voice was amused. "Out for a mornin' stroll?"

"By courtesy of a bunch of Comanches. I was bullwhacking with a wagon train out of Santa Fe for Cheyenne and we had a little Winchester arbitration. They held the high cards." Briefly he explained.

"You'll want a hoss. Ever work cattle?"

"Here and there. D'you need a hand?"

"Forty a month and all you can eat."

"The coffee's a fright," the other rider said. "That dough wrangler never learned to make coffee that didn't taste like strong lye."

That night in camp Jed Asbury got out the papers he had found in the wagon. He read the first letter he opened.

Dear Michael,

When you get this you will know George is dead. He was thrown from a horse near Willow Springs, dying the following day. The home ranch comprises 60,000 acres and the

other ranches twice that. This is to be yours or your heirs if you have married since we last heard from you, if you or the heirs reach the place within one year of George's death. If you do not claim your estate within that time, the property will be inherited by next of kin. You may remember what Walt is like, from the letters.

Naturally we hope you will come at once for we all know what it would be like if Walt took over. You should be around twenty-six now and able to handle Walt, but be careful. He is dangerous and has killed several men.

Things are in good shape now but trouble is impending with Besovi, a neighbor of ours. If Walt takes over, that will certainly happen. Also, those of us who have worked and lived here so long will be thrown out.

Tony Costa

The letter had been addressed to Michael Latch, St. Louis, Missouri. Thoughtfully Jed folded the letter and then glanced through the others. He learned much, yet not enough.

Michael Latch had been the nephew of George Baca, a half-American, half-Spanish rancher who owned a huge *hacienda* in California. Neither Baca nor Tony Costa had ever seen Michael. Nor had the man named Walt, who apparently was the son of George's half-brother. The will was that of Michael's father,

Thomas Latch, and conveyed to Michael the deed to a small California ranch.

From other papers and an unmailed letter, Jed discovered that the younger of the two men he had buried had been Michael Latch. The other dead man and the woman had been Randy and May Kenner. There was mention in a letter of a girl named Arden who had accompanied them.

The Indians must have taken her with them, Jed mused. He considered trying to find her, but dismissed the idea as impractical. Looking for a needle in a haystack would at least be a local job, but trying to find one of many roving bands of Comanches would be well nigh impossible. Nevertheless, he would inform the Army and the trading posts. Often, negotiations could be started, and for an appropriate trade in goods she might be recovered, if still living.

Then he had another idea. Michael Latch was dead. A vast estate awaited him, a fine, comfortable, constructive life, which young Latch would have loved. Now the estate would fall to Walt, whoever he was, unless he, Jed Asbury, took the name of Michael Latch and claimed the estate.

The man who was his new boss rode in from a ride around the herd. He glanced at Jed, who was putting the letters away. "What did you say your name was?"

Only for an instant did Jed hesitate. "Latch," he replied, "Michael Latch."

Warm sunlight lay upon the *hacienda* called Casa Grande. The hounds sprawling in drowsy peace under

58

the smoke trees scarcely opened their eyes when the tall stranger turned his horse through the gate. Many strangers came to Casa Grande, and the uncertainty that hung over the vast ranch had not reached the dogs.

Tony Costa straightened his lean frame from the doorway and studied the stranger from under an eye-shielding hand.

"*Señorita*, someone comes!"

"Is it Walt?" Sharp, quick heels sounded on the flagstoned floor. "What will we do? Oh, if Michael were only here!"

"Today is the last day," Costa said gloomily.

"Look!" The girl touched his arm. "Right behind him! That's Walt Seever!"

"Two men with him. We will have trouble if we try to stop him, *señorita*. He would not lose the ranch to a woman."

The stranger on the black horse swung down at the steps. He wore a flat-crowned black hat and a black broadcloth suit. His boots were almost new and hand-tooled, but when her eyes dropped to the guns, she gasped. "Tony! The guns!"

The young man came up the steps, swept off his hat, and bowed. "You are Tony Costa? The foreman of Casa Grande?"

The other riders clattered into the court, and their leader, a big man with bold, hard eyes, swung down. He brushed past the stranger and confronted the foreman.

"Well, Costa, today this ranch becomes mine, and you're fired!"

"I think not."

All eyes turned to the stranger. The girl's eyes were startled, suddenly cautious. This man was strong, she thought suddenly, and he was not afraid. He had a clean-cut face, pleasant gray eyes, and a certain assurance born of experience.

"If you are Walt," the stranger said, "you can ride back where you came from. This ranch is mine. I am Michael Latch."

Fury struggled with shocked disbelief in the expression on Walt Seever's face. "You? Michael Latch? You couldn't be!"

"Why not?" Jed was calm. Eyes on Seever, he could not see the effect of his words on Costa or the girl. "George sent for me. Here I am."

Mingled with the baffled rage, there was something else in Walt's face, some ugly suspicion or knowledge. Suddenly Jed suspected that Walt knew he was not Michael Latch. Or doubted it vehemently.

Tony Costa had moved up beside him. "Why not? We have expected him. His uncle wrote for him, and after Baca's death I wrote to him. If you doubt it, look at the guns. Are there two such pairs of guns in the world? Are there two men in the world who could make such guns?"

Seever's eyes went to the guns, and Jed saw doubt and puzzlement replace the angry certainty.

"I'll have to have more proof than a pair of guns."

Jed took the letter from his pocket and passed it over. "From Tony. I also have my father's will and other letters."

Walt Seever glanced at the letter and then hurled it into the dust. "Let's get out of here!" He started for his horse.

Jed Asbury watched them go, puzzling over that odd reaction of Walt's. Until Seever saw that letter, he had been positive Jed was not Michael Latch. Now he was no longer sure. But what could have made him so positive in the beginning? What could he know?

The girl was whispering something to Costa. Jed turned, smiling at her. "I don't believe Walt was too happy at my being here," he said.

"No" — Costa's expression was unrevealing — "he isn't. He expected to have this ranch for himself." Costa turned toward the girl. "*Señor* Latch? I would introduce to you *Señorita* Carol James, a . . . a ward of *Señor* Baca's and his good friend."

Jed acknowledged the introduction.

"You must bring me up to date. I want to know all you can tell me about Walt Seever."

Costa exchanged a glance with Carol. "Of course, *señor*. Walt Seever is a *malo hombre, señor*. He has killed several men, is most violent. The men with him were Harry Strykes and Gin Feeley. They are gunmen and believed to be thieves."

Jed Asbury listened attentively, yet wondered about Carol's reaction. Did she suspect he was not Michael Latch? Did she know he was not Latch? If so, why didn't she say something?

He was surprised they had accepted him so readily, for even after he had decided to take the dead man's place he had not been sure he could go through with it.

He had a feeling of guilt and some shame, yet the real Michael Latch was dead, and the only man he was depriving seemed to be a thoroughly bad one whose first action would have been to fire the ranch's foreman, a man whose home had always been this *hacienda*.

He had made a wild ride over rough country to get here in time, but over all that distance he had debated with himself about the rights and the wrongs of his action. He was nobody, a drifter, worker at whatever came to hand, an adventurer, if you will, but not unlike hundreds of others who came and went across the West and more often than not left their bones in the wilderness, their flesh to feed the ancient soil.

He had not known Michael Latch, or what kind of man he had been, but he suspected he had been a good man and a trusted one. Why could he not save the ranch from Walt Seever, find a home for himself at last, and be the kind of man Michael Latch would have been?

All through that wild ride West he had struggled with his conscience, trying to convince himself that what he did was the right thing. He could do Latch no harm, and Costa and Carol seemed pleased to have him here, now that he had arrived. The expression on Seever's face had been worth the ride, if nothing more.

There was something else that disturbed him. That was Walt Seever's odd reaction when he had said he was Michael Latch.

"You say," Jed turned to Carol, "that Seever was sure he would inherit?"

She nodded. "Yes, though until about three months ago he was hating George Baca for leaving the ranch to you. Then suddenly he changed his mind and seemed sure he would inherit, that you would never come to claim your inheritance."

It had been about three months ago that Jed Asbury had come upon the lone wagon and the murdered people, a murder he had laid to Indians. But leaving the corpses with their clothing and the wagon unlooted did not seem like any raiding parties of which he had known. Three people murdered — could Seever have known of that? Was that why he had suddenly been sure he would inherit?

The idea took root. Seever must have known of the killings. If that was so, then the three had not been killed by Indians, and a lot remained to be explained. How did the wagon happen to be alone, so far from anywhere? And what had become of the girl, Arden?

If Indians had not made the attack and carried Arden off, then somebody else had captured her, and wherever she was she would know he was not the real Michael Latch. She would know Jed Asbury for an imposter, but she might also know who the killers were.

Walking out on the wide terrace overlooking the green valley beyond the ranch house, Jed stared down the valley, his mind filled with doubts and apprehensions.

It was a lovely land, well watered and rich. Here, with what he knew of land and cattle, he could carry on the work George Baca had begun. He would do what

Michael Latch would have done, and he might even do it better.

There was danger, but when had he not known danger? And these people at the ranch were good people, honest people. If he did not do more than save the ranch from Seever and his lawless crowd, he would have adequate reason for taking the place of the dead man. Yet he was merely finding excuses for his conduct.

The guns he wore meant something, too. Carol had recognized them, and so had Seever. What was their significance?

He was in deep water here. Every remark he made must be guarded. Even if they had not seen him before, there must be family stories and family tradition of which he knew nothing. There was a movement behind him, and Jed Asbury turned. In the gathering dusk he saw Carol.

"Do you like it?" She gestured toward the valley.

"It's splendid. I have never seen anything prettier. A man could do a lot with land like that. It could be a paradise."

"Somehow you are different than I expected."

"I am?" He was careful, waiting for her to say more.

"You're much more assured than I expected you to be. Mike was quiet, Uncle George used to say. Read a lot, but did not get around much. You startled me by the way you handled Walt Seever."

He shrugged. "A man changes. He grows older, and coming West to a new life makes a man more sure of himself."

64

She noticed the book in his pocket. "What book do you have?" she asked curiously.

It was a battered copy of Plutarch. He was on safe ground here, for on the flyleaf was written: **To Michael, from Uncle George**.

He showed it to her and she said: "It was a favorite of Uncle George's. He used to say that next to the Bible more great men had read Plutarch than any other book."

"I like it. I've been reading it nights." He turned to face her. "Carol, what do you think Walt Seever will do?"

"Try to kill you or have you killed," she replied. She gestured toward the guns. "You had better learn to use those."

"I can, a little."

He dared not admit how well he could use them, for a man does not come by such skill overnight, nor the cool nerve it takes to use them facing an armed enemy. "Seever has counted on this place, has he?"

"He has made a lot of talk." She glanced up at him. "You know, Walt was no blood relation to Uncle George. He was the son of a woman of the gold camps who married George Baca's half-brother."

"I see." Actually Walt Seever's claim was scarcely better than his own. "I know from the letters that Uncle George wanted me to have the estate, but I feel like an outsider. I am afraid I may be doing wrong to take a ranch built by the work of other people. Walt may have more right to it than I. I may be doing wrong to assert my claim."

He was aware of her searching gaze. When she spoke, it was deliberately and as if she had reached some decision.

"Michael, I don't know you, but you would have to be very bad, indeed, to be as dangerous and evil as Walt Seever. I would say that no matter what the circumstances, you should stay and see this through."

Was there a hint that she might know more than she admitted? Yet it was natural that he should be looking for suspicion behind every phrase. Yet he must do that or be trapped.

"However, it is only fair to warn you that you have let yourself in for more than you could expect. Uncle George knew very well what you would be facing. He knew the viciousness of Walt Seever. He doubted you would be clever or bold enough to defeat Seever. So I must warn you, Michael Latch, that, if you do stay, and I believe you should, you will probably be killed."

He smiled into the darkness. Since boyhood he had lived in proximity to death. He was not foolhardy or reckless, for a truly brave man was never reckless. He knew he could skirt the ragged edge of death if need be. He had been there before.

He was an interloper here, yet the man whose place he had taken was dead, and perhaps he could carry on in his place, making the ranch safe for those who loved it. Then he could move on and leave this ranch to Carol and to the care of Tony Costa.

He turned. "I am tired," he said. "I have ridden long and hard to get here. Now I'd like to rest." He paused. "But I shall stay, at least . . ."

★ ★ ★

Jed Asbury was already fast asleep when Carol went into the dining room where Tony Costa sat at the long table. Without him, what would she have done? What could she have done? He had worked with her father for thirty years and had lived on the *hacienda* all his life, and he was past sixty now. He still stood as erect and slender as he had when a young man. And he was shrewd.

Costa looked up. He was drinking coffee by the light of a candle. "For better or worse, *señorita*, it has begun. What do you think now?"

"He told me, after I warned him, that he would stay."

Costa studied the coffee in his cup. "You are not afraid?"

"No. He faced Walt Seever and that was enough for me. Anything is to be preferred to Walt Seever."

"*Sí.*" Costa's agreement was definite. "*Señorita*, did you notice his hands when he faced Seever. They were ready, Carolita, ready to draw. This man has used a gun before. He is a strong man, Carolita."

"Yes, I think you are right. He is a strong man."

For two days nothing happened from the direction of town. Walt Seever and his hard-bitten companions might have vanished from the earth, but on the Rancho Casa Grande much was happening, and Tony Costa was whistling most of the time.

Jed Asbury's formal education was slight, but he knew men, how to lead them, and how best to get results. Above all, he had practical knowledge of handling cattle and of range conditions.

He was up at 5:00 the morning after his discussion with Carol, and, when she awakened, old María, the cook, told her the *Señor* was hard at work in his office. The door was open a crack, and, as she passed by, she glimpsed him deep in the accounts of the ranch. Pinned up before him was a map of the Casa Grande holdings, and, as he checked the disposition of the cattle, he studied the map.

He ate a hurried breakfast and at 8:00 was in the saddle. He ate his next meal at a line camp and rode in long after dark. In two days he spent twenty hours in the saddle.

On the third day he called Costa to the office and sent María to request the presence of Carol. Puzzled and curious, she joined them.

Jed wore a white shirt, black trousers, and the silver guns. His face seemed to have thinned down in just the two days, but, when he glanced at her, he smiled.

"You have been here longer than I and are, in a sense, a partner." Before she could interrupt, he turned to Costa. "I want you to remain as foreman. However, I have asked you both to be here as I plan some changes." He indicated a point on the map. "That narrow passage leads into open country and then desert. I found cattle tracks there, going out. It might be rustlers. A little blasting up in the rocks will close that gap."

"It is a good move," Costa agreed.

"This field . . ." — Jed indicated a large area in a field not far from the house — "must be fenced off. We will plant it to flax."

68

"Flax, *señor?*"

"There will be a good market for it." He indicated a smaller area. "This piece we will plant to grapes, and all that hillside will support them. There will be times when we cannot depend on cattle or horses, so there must be other sources of income."

Carol watched in wonderment. He was moving fast, this new Michael Latch. He had grasped the situation at once and was moving to make changes that Uncle George had only thought about.

"Also, Costa, we must have a roundup. Gather the cattle and cut out all those over four years old, and we'll sell them. I saw a lot of cattle from five to eight years old back there in the brush."

After he had ridden away to study another quarter of the ranch, Carol walked to the blacksmith shop to talk to Pat Flood. He was an old seafaring man with a peg leg who Uncle George had found broke and on the beach in San Francisco and who had proved to be a marvel with tools.

He looked up from under his bushy brows as she stopped at the shop. He was cobbling a pair of boots. Before she could speak, he said: "This here new boss, Latch? Been to sea, ain't he?"

Surprised, she said: "What gave you that idea?"

"Seen him throw a bowline on a bight yesterday. Purtiest job I seen since comin' ashore. He made that rope fast like he'd been doin' it for years."

"I expect many men handle ropes well," she commented.

"Not sailor fashion. He called it a line, too. 'Hand me that line!' he says. Me, I been ashore so long I'm callin' them ropes m'self, but not him. I'd stake my supper that he's walked a deck."

Jed Asbury was riding to town. He wanted to assay the feeling of the townspeople toward the ranch, toward George Baca and Walt Seever. There was a chance he might talk to a few people before they discovered his connection. Also, he was irritated at the delay in the showdown with Seever. His appearance in town might force that showdown or allow Seever an opportunity if he felt he needed one. If there was to be a meeting, he wanted it over with so he could get on with work at the ranch.

He had never avoided trouble. It was his nature to go right to the heart of it, and for this trip he was wearing worn gray trousers, boots, his silver guns, and a battered black hat. He hoped they would accept him as a drifting cowpuncher.

Already, in riding around the ranch and in casual talk with the hands, he had learned a good deal. He knew the place to go in town was the Golden Strike. He tied his horse to the hitching rail and went inside.

Three men loafed at the bar. The big man with the scar on his lip was Harry Strykes, who had ridden with Seever. As Jed stepped to the bar and ordered his drink, a man seated at a table got up and went to Strykes. "Never saw him before," he said.

Strykes went around the man and faced Jed. "So? Cuttin' in for yourself, are you? Well, nobody gets in the way of my boss. Go for your gun or go back to Texas. You got a choice."

"I'm not going to kill you," Jed said. "I don't like your manner, but if you touch that gun, I'll have to blow your guts out. Instead, I'd rather teach you a lesson."

His left hand grabbed Strykes by the belt. He shoved back and then lifted, and his left toe kicked Strykes's foot from under him as Jed lifted on the belt and then let go.

The move caught Strykes unaware, and he hit the floor hard. For an instant he was shaken, but then he came off the floor with a curse.

Jed Asbury had taken up his drink with his left hand, leaning carelessly against the bar. Jed's left foot was on the brass rail, and, as Strykes swung his right fist, Jed straightened his leg, moving himself out from the bar so that the punch missed, throwing Strykes against the bar. As his chest hit the bar, Jed flipped the remainder of his drink into Strykes's eyes.

Moving away from the bar, he made no attempt to hit Strykes, just letting the man paw at the stinging whiskey in his eyes. When he seemed about to get his vision cleared, Jed leaned forward and jerked open Strykes's belt. Strykes's pants slid toward his knees, and he grabbed at them. Jed pushed him with the tips of his fingers. With his pants around his knees Strykes could not stagger, so he fell.

Jed turned to the others in the room. "Sorry to have disturbed you, gentlemen. The name is Mike Latch. If you are ever out to the Casa Grande, please feel free to call."

He walked out of the saloon, leaving laughter behind him as Strykes struggled to get up and pull his pants into place.

Yet he was remembering the man who had stepped up to Strykes, saying he had never seen Jed before. Had that man known the real Mike Latch? If Walt Seever knew of the covered wagon with its three murdered people, he would know Jed Asbury was an impostor and would be searching for a way to prove it. The vast and beautiful acres of Rancho Casa Grande were reason enough.

Riding homeward, he mulled over the problem. There was, of course, a chance of exposure, yet no one might ever come near who could actually identify him.

His brief altercation with Strykes had gotten him nowhere. He had undoubtedly been observed when riding into town, and the stranger must have known the real Latch. Nevertheless, the fight, if such it could be called, might have won a few friends. In the first place he could not imagine a man of Seever's stamp was well liked; in the second he had shown he was not anxious to get into a gun battle. Friends could be valuable in the months to come, and he was not catering to the rowdy element that would be Seever's friends.

Seever, however, would now be spoiling for a fight, and Jed might be killed. He must find a way to give Carol a strong claim on the ranch. Failing in that, he must kill Walt Seever.

Jed Asbury had never killed a man except to protect his own life or those close to him. Deliberately to hunt down and shoot a man was something he had never dreamed of doing, yet it might prove the only way he could protect Carol and Tony Costa. With a shock he realized he was thinking more of Carol than of himself, and he hardly knew her.

Apparently the stranger had known he was not Mike Latch. The next time it might be a direct accusation before witnesses. Jed considered the problem all the way home.

Unknown to Jed, Jim Pardo, one of the toughest hands on the ranch, had followed him into town. On his return, Pardo drew up before the blacksmith shop and looked down at Pat Flood. The gigantic old blacksmith would have weighed well over three hundred pounds with two good legs, and he stood five inches over six feet. He rarely left the shop, as his wooden leg was always giving him trouble.

"He'll do," Pardo said, swinging down.

Flood lit his corncob pipe and waited.

"Had a run-in with Harry Strykes."

Flood drew on the pipe, knowing the story would come.

"Made a fool of Harry."

"Whup him?"

"Not like he should've, but maybe this was worse. He got him laughed at."

"Strykes will kill him for that."

Pardo rolled a cigarette and explained: "If Strykes is smart, he will leave him alone. This here Latch is no greenhorn. He's a man knows what he can do. No other would have handled it like he did. Never turned a hair when Strykes braced him. He's got sand in his gizzard, an' I'm placin' my bets that he'll prove a first-class hand with a shootin' iron. This one's had trouble before."

"He's deep," Flood said, chewing on his pipe stem. "Old George always said Latch was a book reader, an' quiet-like. Well" — Flood was thoughtful — "he's quiet enough, an' he reads books."

Tony Costa learned of the incident from Pardo, and María related the story to Carol. Jed made no reference to it at supper.

Costa hesitated after arising from the table. "Señor, since Señor Baca's death the señorita has permitted me to eat in the ranch house. There was often business to discuss. If you wish, I can . . ."

"Forget it and, unless you're in a hurry, sit down. Your years on the ranch have earned you your place at the table."

Jed took up the pot and filled their cups. "Yesterday I was over in Fall Valley and I saw a lot of cattle with a Bar O brand."

"Bar O? Ah, they try it again. This brand, señor, belongs to a very big outfit. Frank Besovi's ranch. He is a big man, señor, a very troublesome man. Always he tries to move in on that valley, but if he takes that, he will want more. He has taken many ranches, so."

"Take some of the boys up there and throw those cattle off our range."

"There will be trouble, señor."

74

"Are you afraid of trouble, Costa?"

The foreman's face tightened. "No, *señor!*"

"Neither am I. Throw them off."

When the cowpunchers moved out in the morning, Jed mounted a horse and rode along. And there would be trouble. Jed saw that when they entered the valley.

Several riders were grouped near a big man with a black beard. Their horses all carried the Bar O brand.

"I'll talk to him, Costa. I want to hear what Besovi has to say."

"Very bad man," Costa warned.

Jed Asbury knew trouble when he saw it. Besovi and his men had come prepared for a showdown. Jed did not speak; he simply pushed his black against Besovi's gray. Anger flared in the big man's eyes. "What the hell are you tryin' to do?" he roared.

"Tell your boys to round up your Bar O cattle and run them back over your line. If you don't, I'll make you run 'em back, afoot."

"What?" Besovi was incredulous. "You say that to me?"

"You heard me. Give the order."

"I'll see you in hell first!" Besovi shouted.

Jed Asbury knew this could be settled in two ways. If he went for a gun, there would be shooting and men would be killed. He chose the other way.

Acting so suddenly the move was unexpected, he grabbed Besovi by the beard and jerked the rancher sharply toward him, at the same time he kicked the rancher's foot loose from his stirrup, and then shoved hard. Besovi, caught unawares by the sheer unexpected-ness of the attack, fell off his horse, and Jed hit the ground beside him.

Besovi came to his feet, clawing for his gun. "Afraid to fight with your hands?" Jed taunted.

Besovi glared and then unbuckled his gun belts and handed them to the nearest horseman. Jed stripped off his own gun belts and handed them to Costa.

Besovi started toward him with a crab-like movement that made Jed's eyes sharpen. He circled warily, looking the big man over.

Jed was at least thirty pounds lighter than Besovi, and it was obvious the big man had power in those mighty shoulders. But it would take more than power to win this kind of a fight. Jed moved in, feinting to get Besovi to reveal his fighting style. Besovi grabbed at his left wrist, and Jed brushed the hand aside and stiffened a left into his face.

Blood showed, and the Casa Grande men yelled. Pardo, rolling his quid of tobacco in his jaws, watched. He had seen Besovi fight before. The big man kept moving in, and Jed circled, wary. Besovi had some plan of action. He was no wild-swinging, hit-or-miss fighter.

Jed feinted again and then stabbed two lefts to Besovi's face, so fast one punch had barely landed before the other smacked home. Pardo was surprised to see how Besovi's head jerked under the impact.

Besovi moved in, and, when Jed led with another blow, the bigger man went under the punch and, leaping close, encircled Jed with his mighty arms. Jed's leap back had been too slow, and he sensed the power

76

in that grasping clutch. If those huge arms closed around him, he would be in serious trouble, so he kicked up his feet and fell.

The unexpected fall caught Besovi off balance and he lunged over him, losing his grip. Quickly he spun, but Jed was already on his feet. Besovi swung and the blow caught Jed on the cheek bone. Jed took the punch standing, and Pardo's mouth dropped open in surprise. Nobody had ever stood up under a Besovi punch before.

Jed struck then, a left and right that landed solidly. The left opened the gash over Besovi's eye a little wider, and the right caught him on the chin, staggering him. Jed moved in, landing both fists to the face. The big man's hands came up to protect his face and Jed slugged him in the stomach.

Besovi got an arm around Jed and hooked him twice in the face with wicked, short punches. Jed butted him in the face with his head, breaking free.

Yet he did not step back but caught the rancher behind the head with his left hand and jerked his head down to meet a smashing right uppercut that broke Besovi's nose.

Jed pushed him away quickly and hit him seven fast punches before Besovi could get set. Like a huge, blind bear Besovi tried to swing, but Jed ducked the punch and slammed both fists to the body.

Besovi staggered, almost falling, and Jed stepped back. "You've had plenty, Besovi, and you're too good a fighter to kill. I could kill you with my fists, but I'd probably ruin my hands in doing it. Will you take those cattle and get out of here?"

Besovi, unsteady on his feet, wiped the blood from his eyes. "Well, I'll be damned! I never thought the man lived . . . Will you shake hands?"

"I'd never shake with a tougher man or a better one."

Their hands gripped, and suddenly Besovi began to laugh. "Come over to supper some night, will you? Ma's been tellin' me this would happen. She'll be pleased to meet you." He turned to his riders. "The fun's over, boys! Round up our stock an' let's go home."

The big rancher's lips were split; there was a cut over his right eye and another under it. The other eye was swelling shut. There was one bruise on Jed's cheek bone that would be bigger tomorrow, but it wasn't enough to show he had been in a fight.

"Can't figure him," Pardo told Flood later. "Is he scared to use his guns? Or does he just like to fight with his hands?"

"He's smart," Flood suggested. "Look, he's made a friend of Besovi. If he'd beaten him to the ground, Besovi might never have forgiven him. He was savin' face for Besovi just like they do it over China way. And what if he'd gone for his guns?"

"Likely four or five of us might not have made it home tonight."

"That's it. He's usin' his head for something more than a place to hang a hat. Look at it. He's made a friend of Besovi and nobody is shot up."

★   ★   ★

Jed, soaking his battered hands, was not so sure. Besovi might have gone for a gun, or one of his hands might have. He had taken a long gamble and won; next time he might not be so lucky. At least, Rancho Casa Grande had one less enemy and one more friend.

If anything happened to him, Carol would need friends. Walt Seever was ominously quiet, and Jed was sure the man was waiting for proof that he was not Michael Latch. And that gave Jed an idea. It was a game at which two could play.

Carol was saddling her horse when he walked out in the morning. She glanced at him, her eyes hesitating on the bruise. "You seem to have a faculty for getting into trouble," she said, smiling.

He led out the black gelding. "I don't believe in ducking troubles. They just pile up on you. Sometimes they get too big to handle."

"You seem to have made a friend of Besovi."

"Why not? He's a good man, just used to taking in all he can put his hands on, but he'll prove a good neighbor." He hesitated, and then glanced off, afraid his eyes would give him away. "If anything happens to me, you'll need friends. I think Besovi would help you."

Her eyes softened. "Thank you, Mike." She hesitated just a little over the name. "You have already done much of what Uncle George just talked of doing."

Costa was gathering the herd Jed wanted to sell, and Pardo was riding with him. Jed did not ask Carol where she was going, but watched her ride away toward the valley. He threw a saddle on his own horse and cinched up. At the sound of horses' hoofs he turned.

Walt Seever was riding into the yard. With him were Harry Strykes and Gin Feeley. The fourth man was the one he had seen in the saloon who had told Walt he was not Michael Latch. Realizing he wore no guns, Jed felt naked and helpless. There was no one around the ranch house who he knew.

Seever drew rein and rested his hands on the pommel of his saddle. "Howdy! Howdy, Jed!"

No muscle changed on Jed Asbury's face. If trouble came, he was going right at Walt Seever.

"Smart play," Seever said, savoring his triumph. "If it hadn't been for me doubtin' you, you might have pulled it off."

Jed waited, watching.

"Now," Seever said, "your game is up. I suppose I should let you get on your horse an' ride, but we ain't about to."

"You mean to kill me like you did Latch and his friends?"

"Think you're smart, do you? Well, when you said that, you dug your own grave."

"I suppose your sour-faced friend here was one of those you sent to kill Latch," Jed commented. "He looks to be the kind."

"Let me kill him, Walt!" The man with the sour face had his hand on his gun. "Just let me kill him!"

Holding up a hand to stop the other man, Seever said: "What I want to know, is where you got them guns?"

"Out of the wagon, of course. The men you sent to stop Latch before he got here messed up. I'd just gotten away from a passel of Indians and was stark naked. I found clothes in the wagon. I also found the guns."

"About like I figured. Now we'll get rid of you, an' I'll have Casa Grande."

Jed was poised for a break, any kind of a break, and stalling for time. "Thieves like you always overlook important things. The men you sent messed up badly. They were in too much of a hurry and didn't burn the wagon. And what about Arden?"

"Arden? Who the devil is Arden?"

Jed had come a step nearer. They would get him, but he was going to kill Walt Seever. He chuckled. "They missed her, Walt. Arden is a girl. She was with Latch when he was killed."

"A girl?" Seever turned on the other man. "Clark, you never said anything about a girl."

"There wasn't any girl," Clark protested.

"He killed three of them, but she was out on the prairie to gather wild onions or something."

"That's a lie! There was only the three of them!" Clark shouted.

"What about those fancy clothes you threw around in the wagon? Think they were an old woman's clothes?"

Walt was furious. "Damn you, Clark. You said you got all of them."

"There wasn't no girl," Clark protested. "Anyway, I didn't see one."

"There was a girl, Walt, and she's safe. If something goes wrong here, you will have to answer for it. You haven't a chance."

Seever's face was ugly with anger. "Anyway, we've got you. We've got you dead to rights." His hand moved toward his gun, but before Jed Asbury could move a muscle, there was a shot.

From behind Jed came Pat Flood's voice. "Keep your hands away from those guns, Walt. I can shoot the buttons off your shirt with this here rifle, and, in case that ain't enough, I got me a scatter-gun right beside me. Now you gents just unbuckle your belts, real easy now! Your first, Seever!"

Jed dropped back swiftly and picked up the shotgun. The men shed their guns. "Now get off your hosses!" Flood ordered.

They dismounted.

Flood asked: "What you want done with 'em, boss? Should we bury them here or give them a runnin' chance?"

"Let them walk back to town," Jed suggested. "All but Clark. I want to talk to Clark."

Seever started to speak, but the buffalo gun and the shotgun were persuasive. He led the way.

"Let me go!" Clark begged. "They'll kill me!"

Jed gathered the gun belts and walked to the blacksmith shop, behind Clark.

"How much did you hear?" he asked Flood.

"All of it," the big blacksmith replied bluntly, "but my memory can be mighty poor. I judge a man by the way he handles himself, and you've been ridin' for the brand. I ain't interested in anything else."

Jed turned on Clark. "Get this straight. You've one chance to live, and you shouldn't have that. Tell us what happened, who sent you, and what you did." He glanced at Flood. "Take this down, every word."

"I got paper and pencil," Flood said. "I always keep a log."

"All right, Clark, a complete confession and you get your horse and a running start."

"Seever will kill me."

"Make your choice. You sign a confession or you can die right here at the end of a rope behind a runaway horse. Seever's not going to kill anybody, ever again."

Clark hesitated, and then he said: "I was broke in Ogden when Seever found me. I'd knowed him before. He told me I was to find this here wagon that was startin' West from Saint Louis. He said I was to make sure they never got here. I never knew there was a woman along."

"Who was with you?"

"Feller named Quinby and a friend of his'n named Buck Stanton. I met up with 'em in Laramie."

"Buck Stanton?"

At Jed's exclamation, Flood glanced at him: "You know them?"

"I killed Buck's brother Cal. They were crooked gamblers."

"Then you were the man they were huntin'!" Clark exclaimed.

"Where are they now?"

"Comin' this way, I suppose. Seever sent for 'em for some reason. Guess he figured they could come in here and prove you was somebody different than you said."

"Seever ordered the killing?"

"Yes, sir. He surely did."

A few more questions and the confession was signed. "Now get on that horse and get out of here before we change our minds and hang you."

"Do I get my guns?"

"You do not. Get going!"

Clark fairly threw himself into the saddle and left at a dead run.

Flood handed the confession to Jed. "Are you going to use it?"

"Not right now. I'll put it in the safe in the house. If Carol ever needs it, she can use it. If I brought it out now, it would prove that I am not Michael Latch."

"I knew you weren't him," Flood said. "Old George told me a good bit about him, but just seein' you around told me you'd covered a lot more country than he ever did."

"Does Carol know?"

"Don't reckon she does, but then she's a right canny lass."

If Stanton and Quinby were headed West, then Seever must have telegraphed for them to come, and they would certainly ally themselves with Seever against him. As if he did not have trouble enough!

Costa and Jim Pardo rode into the yard, and Costa trotted his horse over to Jed, who was wearing the silver guns now.

"There were many cattle. More than expected. We came to see if the Willow Springs boys can help us."

"Later. Was Miss Carol out with you?"

"No, *señor*. She went to town."

Jed swore. "Flood, you take care of things here. We're riding into town."

Seever would stop at nothing now, and, if Quinby and Stanton had arrived in town, Jed's work would be cut out for him. No doubt Seever had known how to reach them, and it must have been from Stanton that Seever learned his name. A description from Seever would have been enough for Stanton to recognize who he was.

The town lay basking in a warm sun. In the distance the Sierras lifted snow-capped peaks against the blue sky. A man loitering in front of the Golden Strike stepped through the doors as Jed appeared in the street with his Casa Grande cowboys. Walt Seever stepped into the doorway, nonchalant, confident.

"Figured you'd be in. We sort of detained the lady, knowin' that would bring you. She can go loose now that you're where we want you."

Jed stepped down from the saddle. This was a trap, and they had ridden right into it.

"There's a gent in front of the express office, boss," Pardo said.

"Thanks, and watch the windows," Jed suggested. "Upstairs windows."

Jed was watching Seever. Trouble would begin with him. He moved away from his horse. No sense in getting a good animal killed. He did not look to see what Costa and Pardo were doing. They would be doing what was best for them and for what was coming.

"Glad you saved me the trouble of hunting you, Seever," he said.

Seever was on the edge of the boardwalk, a big man looking granite-hard and tough. "Save us both trouble. Folks here don't take to outsiders. They'd sooner have somebody like me runnin' the outfit than a stranger. Shuck your guns, get on your horse, and you can ride out of town."

"Don't do it, boss," Pardo warned. "He'll shoot you as soon as your back is turned."

"The ranch goes to Miss Carol, Seever. You might get me, but I promise you, you will die."

"Like hell!" Seever's hand swept for his gun. "I'll kill . . ."

"Look out!" Pardo yelled.

Jed stepped aside as the rifle roared from the window over the livery barn, and his guns lifted. His first bullet took Walt Seever in the chest; his second went into the shadows behind a rifle muzzle in the barn loft.

Seever staggered into the street, his guns pounding lead into the street. Oblivious of the pounding guns around him, Jed centered his attention on Seever, and, when the man fell, the pistol dribbling from his fingers, Jed looked around, keeping his eyes from this man he had killed, hating the sight of what he had done.

Costa was down on one knee, blood staining the left sleeve of his shirt, but his face was expressionless, his pistol ready.

86

A dead man sprawled over the windowsill above the barn. A soft wind stirred his sandy hair. That would be Stanton. Pardo was holstering his gun. There was no sign of Strykes or Feeley.

"You all right, boss?" Pardo asked.

"All right. How about you?"

Tony Costa was getting to his feet. "Caught one in the shoulder," he said. "It's not bad."

Heads were appearing in doors and windows, but nobody showed any desire to come outside. Then a door slammed down the street, and Carol was running to them.

"Are you hurt?" She caught his arm. "Were you shot?"

He slid an arm around her as she came up to him, and it was so natural that neither of them noticed. "Better get that shoulder fixed up, Costa." He glanced down at Carol. "Where did they have you?"

"Strykes and Feeley were holding me in a house across the street. When Feeley saw you were not alone, he wanted Harry Strykes to leave. Feeley looked out the door and Pat Flood saw him."

"Flood?"

"He followed you in, knowing there'd be trouble. He came in behind them and had me take their guns. He was just going out to help you when the shooting started."

"Carol . . ." He hesitated. "I've got a confession to make. I am not Michael Latch."

"Oh? Is that all? I've known that all the time. You see, I was Michael Latch's wife."

"His what?"

"Before I married him, I was Carol Arden James. He was the only one who ever called me Arden. During the time we were coming West, I was quite ill, so I stayed in the wagon and Clark never saw me at all.

"He convinced Michael there was a wagon train going by way of Santa Fe that would take us through sooner, and, if we could catch them, it would help. It was all a lie to get us away from the rest of the wagons, but Michael listened, as the train we were with was going only as far as Laramie. After we were on the trail, Clark left us to locate the wagon train, as he said. Randy Kenner and Mike decided to camp, and I went over the hill to a small pool to bathe. When I was dressing, I heard shooting, and, believing it was Indians, I crept to the top of a hill so I could see our wagon.

"It was all over. Clark had ridden up with two men and opened fire at once. They'd had no warning, no chance. Randy was not dead when I saw them. One of the men kicked a gun out of his hand . . . he was already wounded . . . and shot him again. There was nothing I could do, so I simply hid."

"But how did you get here?"

"When they left, I did not go back to the wagon. I simply couldn't, and I was afraid they might return. So I started walking back to the wagon train we had left. I hadn't gone far when I found Old Nellie, our saddle mare. She knew me and came right up to me, so I rode her back to the wagon train. I came from Laramie by stage."

"Then you knew all the time that I was faking?"

"Yes, but when you stopped Walt, I whispered to Costa not to say anything."

"He knew as well?"

"Yes. I'd showed him my marriage license, which I always carried with me, along with a little money."

"Why didn't you say something? I was having a battle with my conscience, trying to decide what was right, always knowing I'd have to explain sooner or later."

"You were doing much better with the ranch than Michael could have. Michael and I grew up together and were much more like brother and sister than husband and wife. When he heard from his Uncle George, we were married, and we liked each other."

Suddenly it dawned on Jed that they were standing in the middle of the street and he had his arm around Carol. Hastily he withdrew it.

"Why didn't you just claim the estate as Michael's wife?"

"Costa was afraid Seever would kill me. We had not decided what to do when you appeared."

"What about these guns?"

"My father made them. He was a gunsmith and he had made guns for Uncle George. These were a present to Mike when he started West."

His eyes avoided hers. "Carol, I'll get my gear and move on. The ranch is yours, and with Seever gone you will be all right."

"I don't want you to go."

He thought his ears deceived him. "You . . . what?"

"Don't go, Jed. Stay with us. I can't manage the ranch alone, and Costa has been happy since you've been here. We need you, Jed. I . . . I need you."

"Well," he spoke hesitantly, "there are things to be done and cattle to be sold, and that quarter section near Willow Springs could be irrigated."

Pardo, watching, glanced at Flood. "I think he's going to stay, Pat."

"Sure," Flood said. "Ships an' women, they all need a handy man around the place."

Carol caught Jed's sleeve. "Then you'll stay?"

He smiled. "What would Costa do without me?"

Four Card Draw

When a man drew four cards, he could expect something like this to happen. Ben Taylor had probably been right when he told him his luck had run out. Despite that, he had a place of his own and, come what may, he was going to keep it.

Nor was there any fault to find with the place. From the moment Allen Ring rode his claybank into the valley he knew he was coming home. This was it; this was the place. Here he would stop. He'd been tumbleweeding all over the West now for ten years, and it was time he stopped if he ever did, and this looked like his fence corner.

Even the cabin looked good, although Taylor told him the place had been empty for three years. It looked solid and fit, and, while the grass was waist high all over the valley and up around the house, he could see trails through it, some of them made by unshod ponies, that meant wild horses, and some by deer. Then there were the tracks of a single shod horse, always the same one.

Those tracks always led right up to the door, and they stopped there; yet he could see that somebody with mighty small feet had been walking up to peer into the windows. Why would a person want to look into a window more than once? The window of an empty cabin? He had gone up and looked in himself, and all he saw was a dusty, dark interior with a ray of light from the opposite window, a table, a couple of chairs, and a fine old fireplace that had been built by skilled hands.

"You never built that fireplace, Ben Taylor," Ring had muttered, "you who never could handle anything but a running iron or a deck of cards. You never built anything in your life as fine and useful as that."

The cabin sat on a low ledge of grass backed up against the towering cliff of red rock, and the spring was not more than fifty feet away, a stream that came out of the rock and trickled pleasantly into a small basin before spilling out and winding thoughtfully down the valley to join a larger stream, a quarter of a mile away.

There were some tall spruces around the cabin, and a couple of sycamores and a cottonwood near the spring. Some gooseberry bushes, too, and a couple of apple trees. The trees had been pruned.

"And you never did that, either, Ben Taylor," Allen Ring had said soberly. "I wish I knew more about this place."

Time had fled like a scared antelope, and with the scythe he found in the pole barn he cut off the tall grass around the house, patched up the holes in the cabin where the pack rats had got in, and even thinned out the bushes — it had been several years since they had been touched — and repaired the pole barn.

The day he picked to clean out the spring was the day Gail Truman rode up to the house. He had been putting the finishing touches on a chair bottom he was making when he heard a horse's hoof strike stone, and he straightened up to see the girl sitting on the red pony. She was staring, open-mouthed, at the stacked hay from the grass he had cut and the washed windows of the house. He saw her swing down and run up to the window, and dropping his tools he strolled up.

"Hunting somebody, ma'am?"

She wheeled and stared at him, her wide blue eyes accusing. "What are you doing here?" she demanded. "What do you mean by moving in like this?"

He smiled, but he was puzzled, too. Ben Taylor had said nothing about a girl, especially a girl like this. "Why, I own the place!" he said. "I'm fixing it up so's I can live here."

"You own it?" Her voice was incredulous, agonized. "You couldn't own it! You couldn't. The man who owns this place is gone, and he would never sell it. Never!"

"He didn't exactly sell it, ma'am," Ring said gently. "He lost it to me in a poker game. That was down Texas way."

She was horrified. "In a poker game? Whit Bayly in a poker game? I don't believe it!"

"The man I won it from was called Ben Taylor, ma'am." Ring took the deed from his pocket and opened it. "Come to think of it, Ben did say that, if anybody asked about Whit Bayly, to say that he died down in the Guadaloupes . . . of lead poisoning."

"Whit Bayly is dead?" The girl looked stunned. "You're sure? Oh."

Her face went white and still and something in it seemed to die. She turned with a little gesture of despair and stared out across the valley, and his eyes followed hers. It was strange, Allen Ring told himself, but it was the first time he had looked just that way, and he stood there, caught up by something nameless, some haunting sense of the familiar.

Before him lay the tall grass of the valley, turning slightly now with the brown of autumn, and to his right a dark stand of spruce, standing stiffly, like soldiers on parade, and beyond them the swell of the hill, and farther to the right the hill rolled up and stopped, and beyond lay a wider valley fading away into the vast purple and mauve of distance and here and there spotted with the golden candles of cottonwoods, their leaves bright yellow with nearing cold.

There was no word for this; it was a picture, yet a picture of which a man could only dream and never reproduce.

"It . . . it's beautiful, isn't it?" he said.

She turned on him, and for the first time she seemed really to look at him, a tall young man with a shock of rust-brown hair and somber gray eyes, having about him the look of a rider and the look of a lonely man.

"Yes, it is beautiful. Oh, I've come here so many times to see it, the cabin, too. I think this is the loveliest place I have ever seen. I used to dream about . . ." She stopped, suddenly confused. "Oh, I'm sorry. I shouldn't talk so." She looked at him soberly. "I'd better go. I guess this is yours now."

He hesitated. "Ma'am," he said sincerely, "the place is mine, and, sure enough, I love it. I wouldn't swap this place for anything. But that view, that belongs to no man. It belongs to whoever looks at it with eyes to see it, so you come any time you like, and look all you please." Ring grinned. "Fact is," he said, "I'm aiming to fix the place up inside, and I'm sure no hand at such things. Maybe you could sort of help me. I'd like it kind of homey-like." He flushed. "You see, I sort of lived in bunkhouses all my life and never had no such place."

She smiled with a quick understanding and sympathy. "Of course! I'd love to, only . . ." — her face sobered — "you won't be able to stay here. You haven't seen Ross Bilton yet, have you?"

"Who's he?" Ring asked curiously. He nodded toward the horsemen he saw approaching. "Is this the one?"

She turned quickly and nodded. "Be careful. He's the town marshal. The men with him are Ben Hagen and Stan Brule."

Brule he remembered — but would Brule remember him?

"By the way, my name is Allen Ring," he said, low-voiced.

"I'm Gail Truman. My father owns the Tall T brand."

Bilton was a big man with a white hat. Ring decided he didn't like him and that the feeling was going to be mutual. Brule he knew, so the stocky man was Ben Hagen. Brule had changed but little, some thinner, maybe, but his hatchet face as lean and poisonous as always.

"How are you, Gail?" Bilton said briefly. "Is this a friend of yours?"

Allen Ring liked to get his cards on the table. "Yes, a friend of hers, but also the owner of this place."

"You own Red Rock?" Bilton was incredulous. "That will be very hard to prove, my friend. Also, this place is under the custody of the law."

"Whose law?" Ring wanted to know. He was aware that Brule was watching him, wary but uncertain as yet.

"Mine. I'm the town marshal. There was a murder committed here, and until that murder is solved and the killer brought to justice, this place will not be touched. You have already seen fit to make changes, but perhaps the court will be lenient."

"You're the town marshal?" Allen Ring shoved his hat back on his head and reached for his tobacco. "That's mighty interesting. Howsoever, let me remind you that you're out of town right now."

"That makes no difference." Bilton's voice was sharp. Ring could see that he was not accustomed to being told off, that his orders were usually obeyed. "You will get off this place before nightfall."

"It makes a sight of difference to me," Allen replied calmly. "I bought this place by staking everything I had against it in a poker game. I drew four cards to win, a nine to match one I had and three aces. It was a fool play that paid off. I registered the deed. She's mine, legal. I know of no law that allows a place to be kept idle because there was a murder committed on it. If after all this time it hasn't been solved, I suggest the town get a new marshal."

Ross Bilton was angry, but he kept himself under control. "I've warned you, and you've been told to leave. If you do not leave, I'll use my authority to move you."

Ring smiled. "Now, listen, Bilton. You might pull that stuff on some folks that don't like trouble. You might bluff somebody into believing you had the authority to do this. You don't bluff me, and I simply don't scare . . . do I, Brule?"

He turned on Brule so sharply that the man stiffened in his saddle, his hand poised as though to grab for a gun. The half-breed's face stiffened with irritation, and then recognition came to him. "Allen Ring," he said. "You again."

"That's right, Brule. Only this time I'm not taking cattle through the Indian Nation. Not pushing them by that ratty bunch of rustlers and highbinders you rode with." Ring turned his eyes toward Bilton. "You're the law? And you ride with him? Why, the man's wanted in every county in Texas for everything from murder to horse thieving."

Ross Bilton stared at Ring for a long minute. "You've been warned," he said.

"And I'm staying," Ring replied sharply. "And keep your coyotes away if you come again. I don't like 'em."

Brule's fingers spread and his lips stiffened with cold fury. Ring watched him calmly. "You know better than that, Brule. Wait until my back is turned. If you reach for a gun, I'll blow you out of your saddle."

Stan Brule slowly relaxed his hand, and then wordlessly he turned to follow Bilton and Hagan, who had watched with hard eyes.

Gail Truman was looking at him curiously. "Why, Brule was afraid of you!" she exclaimed. "Who are you, anyway?"

"Nobody, ma'am," he said simply. "I'm no gunfighter, just an *hombre* who ain't got brains enough to scare proper. Brule knows it. He knows he might beat me, but he knows I'd kill him. He was there when I killed a friend of his, Blaze Garden."

"But . . . but then you must be a gunman. Blaze Garden was a killer. I've heard Dad and the boys talk about him."

"No, I'm no gunman. Blaze beat me to the draw. In fact, he got off his first shot before my gun cleared the holster, only he shot too quick and missed. His second and third shots hit me while I was walking into him. The third shot wasn't so bad because I was holding my fire and getting close. He got scared and stepped back, and the fourth shot was too high. Then I shot and I was close up to him then. One was enough. One is always enough if you place it right." He gestured at the place. "What's this all about? Mind telling me?"

"It's very simple, really. Nothing out here is very involved when you come to that. It seems that there's something out here that brings men to using guns much faster than in other places, and one thing stems from another. Whit Bayly owned this place. He was a fixing man, always tinkering and fixing things up. He was a tall, handsome man who all the girls loved . . ."

"You, too?" he asked quizzically.

She flushed. "Yes, I guess so, only I'm only eighteen now, and that was three, almost four years ago. I wasn't very pretty or very noticeable and much too young. Sam Hazlitt was one of the richest men in the country around here, and Whit had a run-in with him over a horse. There had been a lot of stealing going on around, and Hazlitt traced some stock of his to this ranch, or so he claimed. Anyway, he accused Bayly of it, and Whit told him not to talk foolish. Furthermore, he told Hazlitt to stay off of his ranch. Well, folks were divided over who was in the right, but Whit had a lot of friends and Hazlitt had four brothers and clannish as all get out.

"Not long after, some riders from Buck Hazlitt's ranch came by that way and saw a body lying in the yard, right over near the spring. When they came down to have a look, thinking Whit was hurt, they found Sam Hazlitt, and he'd been shot dead . . . in the back. They headed right for town, hunting Whit, and they found him. He denied it, and they were going to hang him, had a rope around his neck, and then I . . . I . . . well, I swore he wasn't anywhere near his ranch all day."

"It wasn't true?" Ring asked keenly, his eyes searching the girl's face. She avoided his eyes, flushing even more.

"Not . . . not exactly. But I knew he wasn't guilty. I just knew he wouldn't shoot a man in the back. I told them he was over to our place, talking with me, and he hadn't time to get back there and kill Sam. Folks didn't like it much. Some of them still believed he killed Sam, and some didn't like it because, despite the way I said it, they figured he was sparking a girl too young for him. I always said it wasn't that. As a matter of fact, I did see Whit over our way, but the rest of it was lies. Anyway, after a few weeks Whit up and left the country."

"I see, and nobody knows yet who killed Sam Hazlitt?"

"Nobody. One thing that was never understood was what became of Sam's account book . . . sort of a tally book, but more than that. It was a sort of record he kept of a lot of things, and it was gone out of his pocket. Nobody ever found it, but they did find the pencil Sam used on the sand nearby. Dad always figured Sam lived long enough to write something, but that the killer stole the book and destroyed it."

"How about the hands? Could they have picked it up? Did Bilton question them about that?"

"Oh, Bilton wasn't marshal then. In fact, he was riding for Buck Hazlitt then. He was one of the hands who found Sam's body."

After the girl had gone, Allen Ring walked back to the house and thought the matter over. He had no intention of leaving. This was just the ranch he wanted, and he intended to live right here, yet the problem fascinated him. Living in the house and looking around the place had taught him a good deal about Whit Bayly. He was, as Gail had said, "a fixing man" for there were many marks of his handiwork aside from the beautifully made fireplace and the pruned apple trees. He was, Ring was willing to gamble, no murderer.

Taylor had said he died of lead poisoning. Who had killed Bayly? Why? Was it a casual shooting over some rangeland argument, or had he been followed from here by someone on vengeance bent? Or someone who thought he might know too much?

"You'll like the place." Taylor had said — that was an angle he hadn't considered before. Ben Taylor had actually seen this place himself! The more sign he read, the more tricky the trail became, and Allen walked outside and sat down against the cabin wall when his supper was finished, and lighted a smoke.

Stock had been followed to the ranch by Sam Hazlitt. If Whit was not the thief, then who was? Where had the stock been driven? He turned his eyes almost automatically toward the Mogollons, the logical place. His eyes narrowed, and he recalled that one night while playing cards they had been talking of springs and water holes, and Ben Taylor had talked about Fossil Springs, a huge spring that roared thousands of gallons of water out of the earth.

"Place a man could run plenty of stock," he had said, and winked, "and nobody the wiser."

Those words had been spoken far away and long ago, and the Red Rock ranch had not yet been put on the table; that was months later. There was, he recalled, a Fossil Creek somewhere north of here. And Fossil Creek might flow from Fossil Springs — perhaps Ben Taylor had talked more to effect than he knew. That had been Texas, and this was Arizona, and a casual bunkhouse conversation probably seemed harmless enough.

"We'll see, Ben," Ring muttered grimly. "We'll see."

Ross Bilton had been one of the Hazlitt hands at the time of the killing, one of the first on the scene. Now he

101

was town marshal but interested in keeping the ranch unoccupied — why? None of it made sense, yet actually it was no business of his. Allen Ring thought that over and decided it was his business in a sense. He now owned the place and lived on it. If an old murder was to interfere with his living there, it behooved him to know the facts. It was a slight excuse for his curiosity.

Morning came and the day drew on toward noon, and there was no sign of Bilton or Brule. Ring had loaded his rifle and kept it close to hand, and he was wearing two guns, thinking he might need a loaded spare, although he rarely wore more than one. Also, inside the cabin door he had his double-barreled shotgun.

The spring drew his attention. At the moment he did not wish to leave the vicinity of the cabin, and that meant it was a good time to clean out the spring. Not that it needed it, but there were loose stones in the bottom of the basin and some moss. With this removed, he would have more water and clearer water. With a wary eye toward the cañon mouth, he began his work.

The sound of an approaching horse drew him erect. His rifle stood against the rocks at hand, and his guns were ready, yet, as the rider came into sight, he saw there was only one man, a stranger. He rode a fine bay gelding and he was not a young man, but thick and heavy with drooping mustache and kind blue eyes. He drew up.

"Howdy," he said affably, yet taking a quick glance around before looking again at Ring. "I'm Rolly Truman, Gail's father."

102

"It's a pleasure," Ring said, wiping his wet hands on a red bandanna. "Nice to know the neighbors." He nodded at the spring. "I picked me a job. That hole's deeper than it looks."

"Good flow of water," Truman agreed. He chewed his mustache thoughtfully. "I like to see a young man with get-up about him, startin' his own spread, willin' to work."

Allen Ring waited. The man was building up to something; what, he knew not. It came then, carefully at first, yet shaping a loop as it drew near. "Not much range here, of course," Truman added. "You should have more graze. Ever been over in Cedar Basin? Or up along the East Verde bottom? Wonderful land up there, still some wild, but a country where a man could really do something with a few white-faced cattle."

"No, I haven't seen it," Ring replied, "but I'm satisfied. I'm not land hungry. All I want is a small piece, and this suits me fine."

Truman shifted in his saddle and looked uncomfortable. "Fact is, son, you're upsetting a lot of folks by being here. What you should do is move."

"I'm sorry," Ring said flatly. "I don't want to make enemies, but I won this place on a four card draw. Maybe I'm a fatalist, but somehow or other I think I should stick here. No man's got a right to think he can draw four cards and win anything, but I did, and in a plenty rough game. I had everything I owned in that pot. Now I got the place."

The rancher sat his horse uneasily, and then he shook his head. "Son, you've sure got to move. There's

103

no trouble here now, but if you stay, she's liable to open old sores and start more trouble than any of us can stop. Besides, how did Ben Taylor get title to this place? Bayly had no love for him. I doubt if your title will stand up in court."

"As to that I don't know," Ring persisted stubbornly. "I have a deed that's legal enough, and I've registered that deed and my brand along with it. I did find out that Bayly had no heirs. So I reckon I'll sit tight until somebody comes along with a better legal claim than mine."

Truman ran his hand over his brow. "Well, I guess I don't blame you much, son. Maybe I shouldn't have come over, but I know Ross Bilton and his crowd, and I reckon I wanted to save myself some trouble as well as you. Gail, she thinks you're a fine young man. In fact, you're the first man she's ever showed interest in since Whit left, and she was a youngster then. It was a sort of hero worship she had for him. I don't want trouble."

Allen Ring leaned on the shovel and looked up at the older man. "Truman," he said, "are you sure you aren't buying trouble by trying to avoid it? Just what's your stake in this?"

The rancher sat very still, his face drawn and pale. Then he got down from his horse and sat on a rock. Removing his hat, he mopped his brow.

"Son," he said slowly, "I reckon I got to trust you. You've heard of the Hazlitts. They are a hard, clannish bunch, men who've lived by the gun most of their lives. Sam was murdered. Folks all know that when they find

104

out who murdered him and why, there's goin' to be plenty of trouble around here. Plenty."

"Did you kill him?"

Truman jerked his head up. "No! No, you mustn't get that idea, but ... well, you know how small ranchers are. There was a sight of rustlin' them days, and the Hazlitts were the big outfit. They lost cows."

"And some of them got your brand?" Ring asked shrewdly.

Truman nodded. "I reckon. Not so many, though. And not only me. Don't get me wrong, I'm not beggin' off the blame. Part of it is mine, all right, but I didn't get many. Eight or ten of us hereabouts slapped brands on Hazlitt stock ... and at least five of us have the biggest brands around here now, some as big almost as the Hazlitts'."

Allen Ring studied the skyline thoughtfully. It was an old story and one often repeated in the West. When the War Between the States ended, men came home to Texas and the Southwest to find cattle running in thousands, unbranded and unowned. The first man to slap on a brand was the owner, with no way he could be contested.

Many men grew rich with nothing more than a wide loop and a running iron. Then the unbranded cattle were gone, the ranches had settled into going concerns, and the great days of casual branding had ended, yet there was still free range, and a man with that same loop and running iron could still build a herd fast.

More than one of the biggest ranchers had begun that way, and many of them continued to brand loose stock wherever found. No doubt that had been true here, and these men like Rolly Truman, good, able men who had fought Indians and built their homes to last, had begun just that way. Now the range was mostly fenced, and ranches had narrowed somewhat, but Ring could see what it might mean to open an old sore now.

Sam Hazlitt had been trailing rustlers — he had found out who they were and where the herds were taken, and he had been shot down from behind. The catch was that the tally book, with his records, was still missing. That tally book might contain evidence as to the rustling done by men who were now pillars of the community and open them to the vengeance of the Hazlitt outfit.

Often Western men threw a blanket over a situation. If a rustler had killed Sam, then all the rustlers involved would be equally guilty. Anyone who lived on this ranch might stumble on that tally book and throw the range into a bloody gun war in which many men now beyond the errors of their youth, with homes, families, and different customs, would die.

It could serve no purpose to blow the lid off the trouble now, yet Allen Ring had a hunch. In their fear of trouble for themselves they might be concealing an even greater crime, aiding a murderer in his escape. There were lines of care in the face of Rolly Truman that a settled, established rancher should not have.

"Sorry," Ring said, "I'm staying. I like this place."

All through the noon hour the tension was building. The air was warm and sultry, and there was a thickening haze over the mountains. There was that hot thickness in the air that presaged a storm. When he left his coffee to return to work, Ring saw three horsemen coming into the cañon mouth at a running walk. He stopped in the door and touched his lips with his tongue.

They reined up at the door, three hard-bitten, hard-eyed men with rifles across their saddle bows. Men with guns in their holsters and men of a kind that would never turn from trouble. These were men with the bark on, lean fanatics with lips thinned with old bitterness.

The older man spoke first. "Ring, I've heard about you. I'm Buck Hazlitt. These are my brothers, Joe and Dolph. There's talk around that you aim to stay on this place. There's been talk for years that Sam hid his tally book here. We figure the killer got that book and burned it. Maybe he did, and, again, maybe not. We want that book. If you want to stay on this place, you stay. But if you find that book, you bring it to us."

Ring looked from one to the other, and he could see the picture clearly. With men like these, hard and unforgiving, it was no wonder Rolly Truman and the other ranchers were worried. The years and prosperity had eased Rolly and his like into comfort and softness, but not these. The Hazlitts were of feudal blood and background.

"Hazlitt," Ring said, "I know how you feel. You lost a brother, and that means something, but if that book is still around, which I doubt, and I find it, I'll decide what to do with it all by myself. I don't aim to start a range war. Maybe there's some things best forgotten. The man who murdered Sam Hazlitt ought to pay."

"We'll handle that," Dolph put in grimly. "You find that book, you bring it to us. If you don't . . ." His eyes hardened. "Well, we'd have to class you with the crooks."

Ring's eyes shifted to Dolph. "Class if you want," he flared. "I'll do what seems best to me with that book. But all of you folks are plumb proddy over that tally book. Chances are nine out of ten the killer found it and destroyed it."

"I don't reckon he did," Buck said coldly, "because we know he's been back here, a-huntin' it. Him an' his girl."

Ring stiffened. "You mean . . . ?"

"What we mean is our figger, not yours." Buck Hazlitt reined his horse around. "You been told. You bring that book to us. You try to buck the Hazlitts and you won't stay in this country."

Ring had his back up. Despite himself he felt cold anger mounting within him. "Put this in your pipe, friend," he said harshly. "I came here to stay. No Hazlitt will change that. I ain't hunting trouble, but if you bring trouble to me, I'll handle it. I can bury a Hazlitt as easy as any other man."

Not one of them condescended to notice the remark. Turning their horses, they walked them down the cañon and out of it into the sultry afternoon. Allen Ring mopped the sweat from his face and listened to the deep rumbling of far-off thunder, growling among the cañons like a grizzly with a toothache. It was going to rain. Sure as shooting, it was going to rain — a regular gully washer.

There was yet time to finish the job on the spring, so he picked up his shovel and started back for the job. The rock basin was nearly cleaned and he finished removing the few rocks and the moss that had gathered. Then he opened the escape channel a little more to insure a more rapid emptying and filling process in the basin into which the trickle of water fell.

The water emerged from a crack in the rocks and trickled into the basin, and, finishing his job, Ring glanced thoughtfully to see if anything remained undone. There was still some moss on the rocks from which the water flowed, and, kneeling down, he leaned over to scrape it away. Pulling away the last shreds, he noticed a space from which a rock had recently fallen. Pulling more moss away, he dislodged another rock, and there, pushed into a niche, was a small black book!

Sam Hazlitt, dying, had evidently managed to shove it back in this crack in the rocks, hoping it would be found by someone not the killer.

Sitting back on his haunches, Ring opened the faded, canvas-bound book. A flap crossed over the page ends, and the book had been closed by a small tongue that slid into a loop of the canvas cover. Opening the book, he saw the pages were stained, but still legible.

The next instant he was struck by lightning. At least, that was what seemed to happen. Thunder crashed, and something struck him on the skull and he tried to rise and something struck again. He felt a drop of rain on

109

his face and his eyes opened wide, and then another blow caught him and he faded out into darkness, his fingers clawing at the grass to keep from slipping down into that velvety, smothering blackness.

He was wet. He turned a little, lying there, thinking he must have left a window open and the rain was . . . His eyes opened and he felt rain pounding on his face and he stared, not at a boot with a California spur, but at dead brown grass, soaked with rain now, and the glistening smoothness of water-worn stones. He was soaked to the hide.

Struggling to his knees, he looked around, his head heavy, his lips and tongue thick. He blinked at a gray, rain-slanted world and at low gray clouds and a distant rumble of thunder following a streak of lightning along the mountaintops.

Lurching to his feet, he stumbled toward the cabin and pitched over the doorsill to the floor. Struggling again to his feet, he got the door closed, and in a vague, misty half world of consciousness he struggled out of his clothes and got his hands on a rough towel and fumblingly dried himself.

He did not think. He was acting purely from vague instinctive realization of what he must do. He dressed again, in dry clothes, and dropped at the table. After a while he sat up and it was dark, and he knew he had blacked out again. He lighted a light and nearly dropped it to the floor. Then he stumbled to the wash basin and splashed his face with cold water. Then he bathed his scalp, feeling tenderly of the lacerations there.

A boot with a California spur. That was all he had seen. The tally book was gone, and a man wearing a new boot with a California-type spur, a large rowel, had taken it. He got coffee on, and, while he waited for it, he took his guns out and dried them painstakingly, wiping off each shell, and then replacing them in his belt with other shells from a box on a shelf.

He reloaded the guns, and then, slipping into his slicker, he went outside for his rifle. Between sips of coffee, he worked over his rifle until he was satisfied. Then he threw a small pack together and stuffed his slicker pockets with shotgun shells.

The shotgun was an express gun and short-barreled. He slung it from a loop under the slicker. Then he took a lantern and went to the stable and saddled the claybank. Leading the horse outside into the driving rain, he swung into the saddle and turned along the road toward Basin.

There was no let-up in the rain. It fell steadily and heavily, yet the claybank slogged along, alternating between a shambling trot and a fast walk. Allen Ring, his chin sunk in the upturned collar of his slicker, watched the drops fall from the brim of his Stetson and felt the bump of the shotgun under his coat.

He had seen little of the tally book, but sufficient to know that it would blow the lid off the very range war they were fearing. Knowing the Hazlitts, he knew they would bring fire and gun play to every home even remotely connected with the death of their brother.

The horse slid down a steep bank and shambled across the wide wash. Suddenly the distant roar that had been in his ears for some time sprang into consciousness and he jerked his head up. His horse snorted in alarm, and Ring stared, open-mouthed, at the wall of water, towering all of ten feet high, that was rolling down the wash toward him.

With a shrill Rebel yell he slapped the spurs to the claybank, and the startled horse turned loose with an astounded leap and hit the ground in a dead run. There was no time to slow for the bank of the wash, and the horse went up, slipped at the very brink, and started to fall back.

Ring hit the ground with both boots and scrambled over the brink, and even as the flood roared down upon them, he heaved on the bridle and the horse cleared the edge and stood, trembling. Swearing softly, Ring kicked the mud from his boots and mounted again. Leaving the raging torrent behind him, he rode on.

Thick blackness of night and heavy clouds lay upon the town when he sloped down the main street and headed the horse toward the barn. He swung down and handed the bridle to the liveryman.

"Rub him down," he said. "I'll be back."

He started for the doors, and then stopped, staring at the three horses in neighboring stalls. The liveryman noticed his glance and looked at him.

"The Hazlitts. They come in about an hour ago, ugly as sin."

Allen Ring stood, wide-legged, staring grimly out the door. There was a coolness inside him now that he recognized. He dried his hands carefully.

"Bilton in town?" he asked.

"Sure is. Playin' cards over to the Mazatzal Saloon."

"He wear Mex spurs? Big rowels?"

The man rubbed his jaw. "I don't remember. I don't know at all. You watch out," he warned. "Folks are on the prod."

Ring stepped out into the street and slogged through the mud to the edge of the boardwalk before the darkened general store. He kicked the mud from his boots and dried his hands again, after carefully unbuttoning his slicker.

Nobody would have a second chance after this. He knew well enough that his walking into the Mazatzal would precipitate an explosion. Only he wanted to light the fuse himself, in his own way.

He stood there in the darkness alone, thinking it over. They would all be there. It would be like tossing a match into a lot of fused dynamite. He wished then that he was a better man with a gun than he was or that he had someone to side him in this, but he had always acted alone and would scarcely know how to act with anyone else.

He walked along the boardwalk with long strides, his boots making hard sounds under the steady roar of the rain. He couldn't place that spur, that boot. Yet he had to. He had to get his hands on that book.

Four horses stood, heads down in the rain, saddles covered with slickers. He looked at them and saw they were of three different brands. The window of the Mazatzal was rain wet, yet standing at one side he glanced within.

The long room was crowded and smoky. Men lined the bar, feet on the brass rail. A dozen tables were crowded with card players. Everyone seemed to have taken refuge here from the rain. Picking out the Hazlitt boys, Allen saw them gathered together at the back end of the room. Then he got Ross Bilton pegged. He was at a table, playing cards, facing the door. Stan Brule was at this end of the bar, and Hagen was at a table against the wall, the three of them making three points of a flat triangle whose base was the door.

It was no accident. Bilton, then, expected trouble, and he was not looking toward the Hazlitts. Yet, on reflection, Ring could see the triangle could center fire from three directions on the Hazlitts as well. There was a man with his back to the door who sat in the game with Bilton. And not far from Hagen, Rolly Truman was at the bar.

Truman was toying with his drink, just killing time. Everybody seemed to be waiting for something. Could it be he they waited upon? No, that was scarcely to be considered. They could not know he had found the book, although it was certain at least one man in the room knew, and possibly others. Maybe it was just the tension, the building up of feeling over his taking over of the place at Red Rock. Allen Ring carefully turned down the collar of his slicker and wiped his hands dry again.

114

He felt jumpy and could feel that dryness in his mouth that always came on him at times like this. He touched his gun butts and then stepped over and opened the door.

Everyone looked up or around at once. Ross Bilton held a card aloft, and his hand froze at the act of dealing, holding still for a full ten seconds while Ring closed the door. He surveyed the room again and saw Ross play the card and say something in an undertone to the man opposite him. The man turned his head slightly, and it was Ben Taylor!

The gambler looked around, his face coldly curious, and for an instant their eyes met across the room, and then Allen Ring started toward him.

There was no other sound in the room, although they could all hear the unceasing roar of the rain on the roof. Ring saw something leap up in Taylor's eyes, and his own took on a sardonic glint.

"That was a good hand you dealt me down Texas way," Ring said. "A good hand!"

"You'd better draw more cards," Taylor said. "You're holdin' a small pair."

Ring's eyes shifted as the man turned slightly. It was the jingle of his spurs that drew his eyes, and there they were, the large rowelled California-style spurs, not common here. He stopped beside Taylor so the man had to tilt his head back to look up. Ring was acutely conscious that he was now centered between the fire of Brule and Hagen. The Hazlitts looked on curiously, uncertain as to what was happening.

"Give it to me, Taylor," Ring said quietly. "Give it to me now."

There was ice in his voice, and Taylor, aware of the awkwardness of his position, got to his feet, inches away from Ring.

"I don't know what you're talking about," he flared.

"No?"

Ring was standing with his feet apart a little, and his hands were breast high, one of them clutching the edge of his raincoat. He hooked with his left from that position, and the blow was too short, too sudden, and too fast for Ben Taylor.

The crack of it on the angle of his jaw was audible, and then Ring's right came up in the gambler's solar plexus and the man's knees sagged. Spinning him around, Ring ripped open his coat with a jerk that scattered buttons across the room. Then from an inside pocket he jerked the tally book.

He saw the Hazlitts start at the same instant that Bilton sprang back from the chair, upsetting it.

"Get him!" Bilton roared. "Get him!"

Ring shoved Taylor hard into the table, upsetting it and causing Bilton to spring back to keep his balance, and at the same instant Ring dropped to a half crouch and, turning left, he drew with a flash of speed and saw Brule's gun come up at almost the same instant, and then he fired!

Stan Brule was caught with his gun just level, and the bullet smashed him on the jaw. The tall man staggered, his face a mask of hatred and astonishment mingled, and then Ring fired again, doing a quick spring around

116

with his knees bent, turning completely around in one leap, and firing as his feet hit the floor. He felt Hagen's bullet smash into him, and he tottered. Then he fired coolly, and, swinging as he fired, he caught Bilton right over the belt buckle.

It was fast action, snapping, quick, yet deliberate. The four fired shots had taken less than three seconds.

Stepping back, he scooped the tally book from the floor where it had dropped and then pocketed it. Bilton was on the floor, coughing blood. Hagen had a broken right arm and was swearing in a thick, stunned voice. Stan Brule had drawn his last gun. He had been dead before he hit the floor.

The Hazlitts started forward with a lunge, and Allen Ring took another step backward, dropping his pistol and swinging the shotgun, still hanging from his shoulder, into firing position.

"Get back!" he said thickly. "Get back or I'll kill the three of you! Back . . . back to where you stood!"

Their faces wolfish, the three stood, lean and dangerous, yet the shotgun brooked no refusal, and slowly, bitterly, and reluctantly the three moved back, step by step.

Ring motioned with the shotgun. "All of you . . . along the wall!"

The men rose and moved back, their eyes on him, uncertain, wary, some of them frightened.

Allen Ring watched them go, feeling curiously light-headed and uncertain. He tried to frown away the pain from his throbbing skull, yet there was a pervading weakness from somewhere else.

"My gosh!" Rolly Truman said. "The man's been shot! He's bleeding!"

"Get back!" Ring said thickly.

His eyes shifted to the glowing potbellied stove, and he moved forward, the shotgun waist high, his eyes on the men who stared at him, awed.

The sling held the gun level, his hand partly supporting it, a finger on the trigger. With his left hand he opened the stove and then fumbled in his pocket.

Buck Hazlitt's eyes bulged. "No!" he roared. "No, you don't!"

He lunged forward, and Ring tipped the shotgun and fired a blast into the floor, inches ahead of Hazlitt's feet. The rancher stopped so suddenly he almost fell, and the shotgun tipped to cover him.

"Back!" Ring said. He swayed on his feet. "Back!" He fished out the tally book and threw it into the flames.

Something like a sigh went through the crowd. They stared, awed as the flames seized hungrily at the opened book, curling around the leaves with hot fingers, turning them brown and then black and to ashes.

Half hypnotized the crowd watched. Then Ring's eyes swung to Hazlitt. "It was Ben Taylor killed him," he muttered. "Taylor, an' Bilton was with him. He . . . he saw it."

"We take your word for it?" Buck Hazlitt demanded furiously.

Allen Ring's eyes widened and he seemed to gather himself. "You want to question it? You want to call me a liar?"

118

Hazlitt looked at him, touching his tongue to his lips. "No," he said. "I figured it was them."

"I told you true," Ring said, and then his legs seemed to fold up under him and he went to the floor.

The crowd surged forward and Rolly Truman stared at Buck as Hazlitt neared the stove. The big man stared into the flames for a minute. Then he closed the door.

"Good!" he said. "Good thing! It's been a torment, that book, like a cloud hangin' over us all!"

The sun was shining through the window when Gail Truman came to see him. He was sitting up in bed and feeling better. It was good to be back on the place again, for there was much to do. She came in, slapping her boots with her quirt and smiling.

"Feel better?" she asked brightly. "You certainly look better. You've shaved."

He grinned and rubbed his jaw. "I needed it. Almost two weeks in this bed. I must have been hit bad."

"You lost a lot of blood. It's lucky you've a strong heart."

"It ain't . . . isn't so strong any more," he said. "I think it's grown mighty shaky here lately."

Gail blushed. "Oh? It has? Your nurse, I suppose?"

"She is pretty, isn't she?"

Gail looked up, alarmed. "You mean, you . . . ?"

"No, honey," he said, "you."

"Oh." She looked at him and then looked down. "Well, I guess . . ."

"All right?"

She smiled then, suddenly and warmly. "All right."

"I had to ask you," he said. "We had to marry."

"Had to? Why?"

"People would talk, a young, lovely girl like you over at my place all the time . . . would they think you were looking at the view?"

"If they did," she replied quickly, "they'd be wrong."

"You're telling me?" he asked.

The Turkeyfeather Riders

Jim Sandifer swung down from his buckskin and stood for a long minute, staring across the saddle toward the dark bulk of Bearwallow Mountain. His was the grave, careful look of a man accustomed to his own company under the sun and in the face of the wind. For three years he had been riding for the B Bar, and for two of those years he had been ranch foreman. What he was about to do would bring an end to that, an end to the job, to the life here, to his chance to win the girl he loved.

Voices sounded inside the ranch house, the low rumble of Gray Bowen's bass and the quick, light voice of his daughter Elaine. The sound of her voice sent a quick spasm of pain across Sandifer's face. Tying the buckskin to the hitch rail, he ducked under it and walked up the steps, his boots sounding loudly on the planed boards, his spurs tinkling lightly.

The sound of his steps brought instant stillness to the group inside and then the quick tattoo of Elaine's feet as she hurried to meet him. It was a sound he would never tire of hearing, a sound that had brought gladness to him such as he had never known before. Yet when her eyes met his at the door, her flashing smile faded.

"Jim! What's wrong?" Then she noticed the blood on his shoulder and the tear where the bullet had ripped his shirt, and her face went white to the lips. "You're hurt!"

"No . . . only a scratch." He put aside her detaining hand. "Wait. I'll talk to your dad first." His hands dropped to hers, and, as she looked up, startled at his touch, he said gravely and sincerely: "No matter what happens now, I want you to know that I've loved you since the day we met. I've thought of little else, believe that." He dropped her hands then and stepped past her into the huge room where Gray Bowen waited, his big body relaxed in a homemade chair of cowhide.

Rose Martin was there, too, and her tall, handsome son Lee. Jim's eyes avoided them for he knew what their faces were like; he knew the quiet serenity of Rose Martin's face, masking a cunning as cold and calculating as her son's flaming temper. It was these two who were destroying the B Bar, they who had brought the big ranch to the verge of a deadly range war by their conniving, a war that could have begun this morning, but for him.

Even as he began to speak, he knew his words would put him right where they wanted him, that when he had finished, he would be through here, and Gray Bowen and his daughter would be left unguarded to the machinations of this woman and her son. Yet he could no longer refrain from speaking. The lives of men depended on it.

Bowen's lips thinned when he saw the blood. "You've seen Katrishen? Had a run-in with him?"

"No." Sandifer's eyes blazed. "There's no harm in Katrishen if he's left alone. No trouble unless we make it. I ask you to recall, Gray, that for two years we've lived at peace with the Katrishens. We have had no trouble until the last three months." He paused, hoping the idea would soak in that trouble had begun with the coming of the Martins. "He won't give us any trouble if we leave him alone."

"Leave him alone to steal our range!" Lee Martin flared.

Sandifer's eyes swung. "Our range? Are you now a partner in the B Bar?"

Lee smiled, covering his slip. "Naturally, as I am a friend of Mister Bowen's, I think of his interests as mine.

Bowen waved an impatient hand. "That's no matter. What happened?"

Here it was, then. The end of all his dreaming, his planning, his hoping. "It wasn't Katrishen. It was Klee Mont."

"Who?" Bowen came out of his chair with a lunge, veins swelling. "Mont shot you? What for? Why, in heaven's name?"

"Mont was over there with the Mello boys and Art Dunn. He had gone over to run the Katrishens off their Iron Creek holdings. If they had tried that, they would have started a first-class range war with no holds barred. I stopped them."

Rose Martin flopped her knitting in her lap and glanced up at him, smiling smugly. Lee began to roll a smoke, one eyebrow lifted. This was what they had wanted, for he alone had blocked them here. The others the Martins could influence, but not Jim Sandifer.

Bowen's eyes glittered with his anger. He was a choleric man, given to sudden bursts of fury, a man who hated being thwarted and who was impatient of all restraint. "You stopped them? Did they tell you whose orders took them over there? Did they?"

"They did. I told them to hold off until I could talk with you, but Mont refused to listen. He said his orders had been given him and he would follow them to the letter."

"He did right!" Bowen's voice boomed in the big room. "Exactly right! And you stopped them? You countermanded my orders?"

"I did." Sandifer laid it flatly on the line. "I told them there would be no burning or killing while I was foreman. I told them they weren't going to run us into a range war for nothing."

Gray Bowen balled his big hands into fists. "You've got a gall, Jim. You know better than to countermand an order of mine. And you'll leave me to decide what range I need. Katrishen's got no business on Iron Creek, an' I told him so. Told him to get off an' get out. As for this range war talk, that's foolishness. He won't fight."

"Putting them off would be a very simple matter," Lee Martin interposed quietly. "If you hadn't interfered, Sandifer, they would be off now and the whole matter settled."

"Settled nothing!" Jim exploded. "Where did you get this idea that Bill Katrishen could be pushed around?

The man was an officer in the Army during the war, and he's fought Indians on the plains."

"You must be a great friend of his," Rose Martin said gently. "You know so much about him."

The suggestion was there, and Gray Bowen got it. He stopped in his pacing, and his face was like a rock. "You been talkin' with Katrishen? You sidin' that outfit?"

"This is my outfit. I ride for the brand," Sandifer replied. "I know Katrishen, of course. I've talked to him."

"And to his daughter?" Lee suggested, his eyes bright with malice. "With his pretty daughter?"

Out of the tail of his eye Jim saw Elaine's head come up quickly, but he ignored Lee's comment. "Stop and think," he said to Bowen. "When did this trouble start? When Missus Martin and her son came here. You got along fine with Katrishen until then. They've been putting you up to this."

Bowen's eyes narrowed. "That will be enough of that!" he said sharply. He was really furious now, not the flaring, hot fury that Jim knew so well, but a cold, hard anger that nothing could touch. For the first time Jim realized how futile any argument was going to be. Rose Martin and her son had insinuated themselves too much and too well into the picture of Gray Bowen's life.

"You wanted my report," Sandifer said quietly. "Mont wouldn't listen to my arguments for time. He said he had his orders and would take none from me. I told him then that if he rode forward it was against my gun. He laughed at me, then reached for his gun. I shot him."

Gray Bowen's widened eyes expressed his amazement. "You shot Mont? You beat him to the draw?"

"That's right. I didn't want to kill him, but I shot the gun out of his hand and held my gun on him for a minute to let him know what it meant to be close to death. Then I started them back here."

Bowen's anger was momentarily swallowed by his astonishment. He recalled suddenly that in the three years Sandifer had worked for him there had been no occasion for him to draw a gun in anger. There had been a few brushes with Apaches and one with rustlers, but all rifle work. Klee Mont was a killer with seven known killings on his record and had been reputed to be the fastest gun hand west of the Rio Grande.

"It seems peculiar," Mrs Martin said composedly, "for you to turn your gun on men who ride for Mister Bowen, taking sides against him. No doubt you meant well, but it does seem strange."

"Not if you know the Katrishens," Jim replied grimly. "Bill was assured he could settle on that Iron Creek holding before he moved in. He was told that we made no claim on anything beyond Willow and Gilita Creeks."

"Who," Lee insinuated, "assured him of that?"

"I did," Jim said coolly. "Since I've been foreman, we've never run any cattle beyond that boundary. Iron Mesa is a block that cuts us off from the country south of there, and the range to the east is much better and is open for us clear to Beaver Creek and south to the Middle Fork."

"So you decide what range will be used? I think for a hired hand you take a good deal of authority. Personally I'm wondering how much your loyalty is divided. Or if it is divided. It seems to me you act more as a friend of the Katrishens . . . or their daughter."

Sandifer took a step forward. "Martin," he said evenly, "are you aiming to say that I'd double-cross the boss? If you are, you're a liar."

Bowen looked up, a chill light in his eyes that Sandifer had never seen there before. "That will be all, Jim. You better go."

Sandifer turned on his heel and strode outside.

When Sandifer walked into the bunkhouse, the men were already back. The room was silent, but he was aware of the hatred in the cold, blue eyes of Mont as he lay sprawled in his bunk. His right hand and wrist were bandaged. The Mello boys snored in their bunks, while Art Dunn idly shuffled cards at the table. These were the new hands, hired since the coming of the Martins. Only three of the older hands were in, and none of them spoke.

"Hello . . . lucky." Mont rolled up on his elbow. "Lose your job?"

"Not yet," Jim said shortly, aware that his remark brought a fleeting anger to Mont's eyes.

"You will," Mont assured him. "If you are in the country when this hand gets well, I'll kill you."

Jim Sandifer laughed shortly. He was aware that the older hands were listening, although none would have guessed it without knowing them.

"You called me lucky, Klee. It was you who were lucky in that I didn't figure on killing you. That was no miss. I aimed for your gun hand. Furthermore, don't try pulling a gun on me again. You're too slow."

"Slow?" Mont's face flamed. He reared up in his bunk. "Slow? Why, you two-handed bluffer!"

Sandifer shrugged. "Look at your hand," he said calmly. "If you don't know what happened, I do. That bullet didn't cut your thumb off. It doesn't go up your hand or arm. The wound runs across your hand."

They all knew what he meant. Sandifer's bullet must have hit his hand as he was in the act of drawing and before the gun came level, indicating that Sandifer had beaten Mont to the draw by a safe margin. That Klee Mont realized the implication was plain, for his face darkened and then paled around the lips. There was pure hatred in his eyes when he looked up at Sandifer.

"I'll kill you," he said viciously. "I'll kill you."

As Sandifer started outside, Rep Dean followed him. With Grimes and Sparkman, he was one of the older hands.

"What's come over this place, Jim? Six months ago there wasn't a better spread in the country." Sandifer did not reply, and Dean built a smoke. "It's that woman," he said. "She twists the boss around her little finger. If it wasn't for you, I'd quit, but I'm thinkin' that there's nothin' she wouldn't like better than for all of the old hands to ask for their time."

128

Sparkman and Grimes had followed them from the bunkhouse. Sparkman was a lean-bodied Texan with some reputation as an Indian fighter.

"You watch your step," Grimes warned. "Next time Mont will back-shoot you!"

They talked among themselves, and, as they conversed, Sandifer ran his thoughts over the developments of the past few months. He had heard enough of Mrs Martin's sly, insinuating remarks to understand how she had worked Bowen up to ordering Katrishen driven off, yet there was no apparent motive. It seemed obvious that the woman had her mind set on marrying Gray Bowen, but for that it was not essential that any move be made against the Katrishens.

Sandifer's limitation of the B Bar range had been planned for the best interests of the ranch. The range they now had in use was bounded by streams and mountain ranges and was rich in grass and water, a range easily controlled with a small number of hands and with little danger of loss from raiding Indians, rustlers, or varmints. His willingness to have the Katrishens move in on Iron Creek was not without the B Bar in mind. He well knew that range lying so much out of the orbit of the ranch could not be long held tenantless, and the Katrishens were stable, honest people who would make good neighbors and good allies. Thinking back, he could remember almost to the day when the first rumors began to spread, and most of them had stemmed from Lee Martin himself. Later, one of the Mello boys had come in with a bullet hole in the crown of his hat and a tale of being fired on from Iron Mesa.

"What I can't figure out," Grimes said, "is what that no-account Lee Martin would be doin' over on the Turkeyfeather."

Sandifer turned his head. "On the Turkeyfeather? That's beyond Iron Mesa. Why, that's clear over the other side of Katrishen's."

"Sure enough. I was huntin' that brindle steer who's always leadin' stock off into the cañons when I seen Martin fordin' the Willow. He was ridin' plumb careful, an' he sure wasn't playin' no tenderfoot then. I was right wary of him, so I took in behind an' trailed him over to that rough country near Turkeyfeather Pass. Then I lost him."

The door slammed up at the house, and they saw Lee Martin come down the steps and start toward them. It was dusk, but still light enough to distinguish faces. Martin walked up to Sandifer.

"Here's your time." He held out an envelope. "You're through."

"I'll want that from Bowen himself," Sandifer replied stiffly.

"He doesn't want to see you. He sent this note." Martin handed over a sheet of the coarse brown paper on which Bowen kept his accounts. On it, in Bowen's hand, was his dismissal.

I won't have a man who won't obey orders. Leave tonight.

130

Sandifer stared at the note, which he could barely read in the dim light. He had worked hard for the B Bar, and this was his answer.

"All right," he said briefly. "Tell him I'm leaving. It won't take any great time to saddle up."

Martin laughed. "That won't take time, either. You'll walk out. No horse leaves this ranch."

Jim turned back, his face white. "You keep out of this, Martin. That buckskin is my own horse. You get back in your hole and stay there."

Martin stepped closer. "Why, you cheap bigmouth!"

The blow had been waiting for a long time, but it came fast now. It was a smashing left that caught Martin on the chin and spilled him on his back in the dust. With a muttered curse, Martin came off the ground and rushed, but Sandifer stepped in, blocking a right and whipping his own right into Lee's mid-section. Martin doubled over, and Jim straightened him with a left uppercut, and then knocked him crashing into the corral fence.

Abruptly Sandifer turned and threw the saddle on the buckskin.

"Dammit, I'm quittin', too!" Sparkman said.

"An' me!" Grimes snapped. "I'll be dog-goned if I'll work here now."

Heavily Martin got to his feet. His white shirt was bloody, and they could vaguely see a blotch of blood over the lower part of his face. He limped away, muttering.

"Sparky," Jim said, low-voiced, "don't quit. All of you stay on. I reckon this fight ain't over, an' the boss may need a friend. You stick here. I'll not be far off."

Sandifer had no plan, yet it was Lee Martin's ride to the Turkeyfeather that puzzled him most, and almost of its own volition his horse took that route. As he rode, he turned the problem over and over in his mind, seeking for a solution, yet none appeared that was satisfactory. Revenge for some old grudge against the Katrishens was considered and put aside; he could not but feel that whatever the reason for the plotting of the Martins, there had to be profit in it somewhere.

Certainly there seemed little to prevent Rose Martin from marrying Gray Bowen if she wished. The old man was well aware that Elaine was a lovely, desirable girl. The cowhands and other male visitors who came to call for one excuse or another were evidence of that. She would not be with him long, and, if she left, he was faced with the dismal prospect of ending his years alone. Rose Martin was a shrewd woman and attractive for her years, and she knew how to make Gray comfortable and how to appeal to him. Yet, obviously, there was something more in her mind than this, and it was that something more in which Sandifer was interested.

Riding due east, Jim crossed Iron Mesa and turned west by south through the broken country. It was very late, and vague moonlight filtered through the yellow pine and fir that guarded the way he rode with their tall columns. Twice he halted briefly, feeling a strange uneasiness, yet listen as he might, he could detect no alien sound, nothing but the faint stirring of the slight breeze through the needles of the pines and the occasional rustle of a blown leaf. He rode on, but now

132

he avoided the bright moonlight and kept more to the deep shadows under the trees.

After skirting the end of the Jerky Mountains, he headed for Turkeyfeather Pass. Somewhere off to his left, lost against the blackness of the ridge shadow, a faint sound came to him. He drew up, listening. He did not hear it again, yet his senses could not have lied. It was the sound of a dead branch scraping along leather, such a sound as might be made by a horseman riding through brush.

Sliding his Winchester from its scabbard, he rode forward, every sense alert. His attention was drawn to the buckskin, whose ears were up and who, when he stopped, lifted his head and stared off toward the darkness. Sandifer started the horse forward, moving easily.

To the left towered the ridge of Turkeyfeather Pass, lifting all of five hundred feet above him, black, towering, ominous in the moonlight. The trees fell away, massing their legions to right and left, but leaving before him an open glade, grassy and still. Off to the right Iron Creek hustled over the stones, whispering wordless messages to the rocks on either bank. Somewhere a quail called mournfully into the night, and the hoofs of the buckskin made light whispering sounds as they moved through the grass at the edge of the glade.

Jim drew up under the trees near the creek and swung down, warning the buckskin to be still. Taking his rifle, he circled the glade under the trees, moving like a prowling wolf. Whoever was over there was stalking him, watching a chance to kill him or perhaps

133

only following to see where he went. In any case, Jim meant to know who and why.

Suddenly he heard a vague sound before him, a creak of saddle leather. Freezing in place, he listened and heard it again, followed by the crunch of gravel. Then he caught the glint of moonlight on a rifle barrel and moved forward, shifting position to get the unseen man silhouetted against the sky. Sandifer swung his rifle.

"All right," he said calmly, "drop that rifle and lift your hands. I've got you dead to rights."

As he spoke, the man was moving forward, and instantly the fellow dived headlong. Sandifer's rifle spat fire, and he heard a grunt, followed by a stab of flame. A bullet whipped past his ear. Shifting ground on cat feet, Jim studied the spot carefully.

The man lay in absolute darkness, but listening he could hear the heavy breathing that proved his shot had gone true. He waited, listening for movement, but there was none. After a while the breathing grew less and he took a chance.

"Better give up!" he said. "No use dying there!"

There was silence and then a slight movement of gravel. Then a six-shooter flew through the air to land in the open space between them.

"What about that rifle?" Sandifer demanded cautiously.

"Lost . . . for God's sake, help . . . me!"

There was no mistaking the choking sound. Jim Sandifer got up and, holding his rifle on the spot where the voice had sounded, crossed into the shadows. As it was, he almost stumbled over the wounded man before he saw him. It was Dan Mello, and the heavy slug had gone into his body but seemed not to have emerged.

Working swiftly, Jim got the wounded man into an easier position and carefully pulled his shirt away from the wound. There was no mistaking the fact that Dan Mello was hit hard. Jim gave the wounded man a drink, and then hastily built a fire to work by. His guess that the bullet had not emerged proved true, but, moving his hand gently down the wounded man's back, he could feel something hard near his spine. When he straightened, Mello's eyes sought his face.

"Don't you move," Sandifer warned. "It's right near your spine. I've got to get a doctor."

He was worried, knowing little of such wounds. The man might be bleeding internally.

"No, don't leave me," Mello pleaded. "Some varmint might come." The effort of speaking left him panting.

Jim Sandifer swore softly, uncertain as to his proper course. He had little hope that Mello could be saved, even if he rode for a doctor. The nearest one was miles away, and movement of the wounded man would be very dangerous. Nor was Mello's fear without cause, for there were mountain lions, wolves, and coyotes in the area, and the scent of blood was sure to call them.

"Legs . . . gone," Mello panted. "Can't feel nothing."

"Take it easy," Jim advised. The nearest place was Bill Katrishen's, and Bill might be some hand with a wounded man. He said as much to Mello. "Can't be more'n three, four miles," he added. "I'll give you back your gun and build up the fire."

"You . . . you'll sure come back?" Mello pleaded.

"What kind of coyote do you think I am?" Sandifer asked irritably. "I'll get back as soon as ever I can." He looked down at him. "Why were you gunning for me? Mont put you up to it?"

Mello shook his head. "Mont, he . . . he ain't . . . bad. It's that Martin . . . you watch. He's pizen mean."

Leaving the fire blazing brightly, Jim returned to his buckskin and jumped into the saddle. The moon was higher now, and the avenues through the trees were like roads, eerily lighted. Touching a spur to the horse, Jim raced through the night, the cool wind fanning his face. Once a deer scurried from in front of him and then bounded off through the trees, and once he thought he saw the lumbering shadow of an old grizzly.

The Katrishen log cabin and pole corrals lay bathed in white moonlight as he raced his horse into the yard. The drum of hoofs upon the hard-packed earth and his call brought movement and an answer from inside: "Who is it? What's up?"

Briefly he explained, and after a minute the door opened.

"Come in, Jim. Figured I heard a shot a while back. Dan Mello, you say? He's a bad one."

Hurrying to the corral, Jim harnessed two mustangs and hitched them to the buckboard. A moment later Bill Katrishen, tall and gray-haired, came from the cabin, carrying a lantern in one hand and a black bag in the other.

"I'm no medical man," he said, "but I fixed a sight of bullet wounds in my time." He crawled into the buckboard, and one of his sons got up beside him.

136

Led by Sandifer, they started back over the way he had come.

Mello was still conscious when they stopped beside him. He looked unbelievingly at Katrishen.

"You came?" he said. "You knowed who . . . who I was?"

"You're hurt, ain't you?" Katrishen asked testily. Carefully he examined the man, and then sat back on his heels. "Mello," he said, "I ain't one for foolin' a man. You're plumb bad off. That bullet seems to have slid off your hip bone an' tore right through you. If we had you down to the house, we could work on you a durned sight better, but I don't know whether you'd make it or not."

The wounded man breathed heavily, staring from one to the other. He looked scared, and he was sweating, and under it his face was pale.

"What you think," he panted, "all right . . . with me."

"The three of us can put him on them quilts in the back of the buckboard. Jim, you slide your hands under his back."

"Hold up." Mello's eyes wavered, and then focused on Jim. "You watch . . . Martin. He's plumb . . . bad."

"What's he want, Mello?" Jim said. "What's he after?"

"G . . . old," Mello panted, and then suddenly he relaxed.

"Fainted," Katrishen said. "Load him up."

All through the remainder of the night they worked over him. It was miles over mountain roads to Silver City and the nearest doctor, and little enough that he could do once he got there. Shortly before the sun lifted, Dan Mello died.

Bill Katrishen got up from beside the bed, his face drawn with weariness. He looked across the body of Dan Mello at Sandifer.

"Jim, what's this all about? Why was he gunning for you?"

Hesitating only a moment, Jim Sandifer explained the needling of Gray Bowen by Rose Martin, the undercover machinations of her and her tall son, the hiring of the Mellos at their instigation and of Art Dunn and Klee Mont. Then he went on to the events preceding his break with the B Bar. Katrishen nodded thoughtfully, but obviously puzzled.

"I never heard of the woman, Jim. I can't figure why she'd have it in for me. What did Mello mean when he said Martin was after gold?"

"You've got me. I know they are money hungry, but the ranch is . . ." He stopped, and his face lifted, his eyes narrowing. "Bill, did you ever hear of gold around here?"

"Sure, over toward Cooney Cañon. You know, Cooney was a sergeant in the Army, and after his discharge he returned to hunt for gold he located while a soldier. The Apaches finally got him, but he had gold first."

"Maybe that's it. I want a fresh horse, Bill."

"You get some sleep first. The boys an' I'll take care of Dan. Kara will fix breakfast for you."

The sun was high when Jim Sandifer rolled out of his bunk and stumbled sleepily to the door to splash his face in cold water poured from a bucket into the tin basin. Kara heard him moving and came to the door, walking carefully and lifting her hand to catch the doorjamb. "Hello, Jim? Are you rested? Dad and the boys buried Dan Mello over on the knoll."

Jim smiled at her reassuringly. "I'm rested, but after I eat, I'll be ridin', Kara." He looked up at the slender girl with the rusty hair and pale freckles. "You keep the boys in, will you? I don't want them to be where they could be shot at until I can figure a way out of this. I'm going to maintain peace in this country or die trying."

"You're a good man, Jim," the girl said. "This country needs more like you."

Sandifer shook his head somberly. "Not really a good man, Kara, just a man who wants peace and time to build a home. I reckon I've been as bad as most, but this is a country for freedom and a country for things to be done. We can't do it when we are killing each other."

The buckskin horse was resting, but the iron gray that Katrishen had provided was a good mountain horse. Jim Sandifer pulled his gray hat low over his eyes and squinted against the sun. He liked the smell of pine needles, the pungent smell of sage. He moved carefully, searching the trail for the way Lee Martin's horse had gone the day Grimes had followed him.

Twice he lost the trail and then found it only to lose it finally in the sand of a wash. The area covered by the sand was small, a place where water had spilled down a steep mountainside, eating out a raw wound in the cliff, yet there the trail vanished. Dismounting, Sandifer's careful search disclosed a brushed-over spot near the

139

cliff and then a chafed spot near the cliff and then a chafed place on a small tree. Here Lee Martin had tied his horse, and from here he must have gone on foot.

It was a small rock, only half as big as his fist, that was the telltale clue. The rock showed where it had lain in the earth but had been recently rolled aside. Moving close, he could see that the stone had rolled from under a clump of brush; the clump rolled easily under his hand. Then he saw that, although the roots were still in the soil, at some time part of it had been pulled free, and the clump had been rolled over to cover an opening no more than a couple of feet wide and twice as high. It was a man-made tunnel, but one not recently made.

Concealing the gray in the trees some distance off, Sandifer walked back to the hole, stared around uneasily, and then ducked his head and entered. Once he was inside, the tunnel was higher and wider, and then it opened into a fair-size room. Here the ore had been stoped out, and he looked around, holding a match high. The light caught and glinted upon the rock, and moving closer he picked up a small chunk of rose quartz seamed with gold.

Pocketing the sample, he walked farther in until he saw a black hole, yawning before him, and beside it lay a notched pole such as the Indians had used in Spanish times to climb out of mine shafts. Looking over into the hole, he saw a longer pole reaching down into the darkness. He peered over, and then straightened. This, then, was what Dan Mello had meant. The Martins wanted gold.

140

The match flickered out, and, standing there in the cool darkness, he thought it over and understood. This place was on land used, and probably claimed, by Bill Katrishen, and it could not be worked unless he were driven off. But could Sandifer make Gray Bowen believe him? What would Lee do if his scheme was exposed? Why had Mello been so insistent that Martin was dangerous?

He bent over and started into the tunnel exit, and then stopped. Kneeling just outside were Lee Martin, Art Dunn, and Jay Mello. Lee had a shotgun pointed at Jim's body. Jim jerked back around the corner of stone even as the shotgun thundered.

"You dirty, murdering rat!" he yelled. "Let me out in the open and try that!"

Martin laughed. "I wouldn't think of it! You're right where I want you now, an' you'll stay there!"

Desperately Jim stared around. Martin was right. He was bottled up now. He drew his gun, wanting to chance a shot at Martin while yet there was time, but when he stole a glance around the corner of the tunnel, there was nothing to be seen. Suddenly he heard a sound of metal striking stone, a rattle of rock, and then a thunderous crash, and the tunnel was filled with dust, stifling and thick. Lee Martin had closed off the tunnel mouth, and he was entombed alive!

Jim Sandifer leaned back against the rock wall of the stope and closed his eyes. He was frightened. He was frightened with a deep, soul-shaking fear, for this was something against which he could not fight, these walls of living rock around him, and the dead débris of the

141

rock-choked tunnel. Had there been time and air, a man might work out an escape, but there was so little time, so little air. He was buried alive.

Slowly the dust settled from the heavy air. Saving his few matches, he got down on his knees and crawled into the tunnel, but there was barely room enough. Mentally he tried to calculate the distance out, and he could see that there was no less than fifteen feet of rock between him and escape — not an impossible task if more rock did not slide down from above. Remembering the mountain, he knew that above the tunnel mouth it was almost one vast slide. He could hear nothing, and the air was hot and close.

On his knees he began to feel his way around, crawling until he reached the tunnel and the notched pole. Here he hesitated, wondering what the darkness below would hold. Water, perhaps? Or even snakes? He had heard of snakes taking over old mines, and once, crawling down the ladder into an old shaft, he had seen an enormous rattler, the biggest he had ever seen, coiled about the ladder just below him. Nevertheless, he began to descend — down, down into the abysmal blackness below him. He seemed to have climbed down an interminable distance when suddenly his boot touched rock.

Standing upright, one hand on the pole, he reached out. His hand found rock on three sides, on the other only empty space. He turned in that direction and ran smack into the rock wall, knocking sparks from his skull. He drew back, swearing, and found the tunnel. At the same time, his hand touched something else, a sort of ledge in the corner of the rock, and on the ledge — his heart gave a leap. Candles!

Quickly he got out a match and lit the first one. Then he walked into the tunnel. Here was more of the rose quartz, and it was incredibly seamed with gold. Lee Martin had made a strike. Rather, studying the walls, he had perhaps found an old Spanish working, although work had been done here within the last few weeks. Suddenly Jim saw a pick and he grinned. There might yet be a way out. Yet a few minutes of exploration sufficed to indicate that there was no other opening. If he was to go out, it must be by the way he came.

Taking the candles with him, he climbed the notched pole and stuck a lighted candle on a rock. Then, with a pick at his side, he started to work at the debris choking the tunnel. He lifted a rock and moved it aside, then another.

An hour later, soaked with sweat, he was still working away, pausing each minute or so to examine the hanging wall. The tunnel was cramped, and the work moved slowly ahead, for every stone removed had to be shoved back into the stope behind him. He reached the broken part overhead and, when he moved a rock, more slid down. He worked on, his breath coming in great gasps, sweat dripping from his face and neck to his hands.

A new sound came to him, a faint tapping. He held still, listening, trying to quiet his breathing and the pound of his heart. Then he heard it again, an unmistakable tapping!

143

Grasping his pick, he tapped three times, then an interval, then three times again. Then he heard somebody pull at the rocks of the tunnel, and his heart pounded with exultation. He had been found!

How the following hours passed Sandifer never quite knew, but, working feverishly, he fought his way through the border of time that divided him from the outer world and the clean, pine-scented air. Suddenly a stone was moved and an arrow of light stabbed the darkness, and with it came the cool air he wanted. He took a deep breath, filling his lungs with air so liquid it might almost be water, and then he went to work, helping the hands outside to enlarge the opening. When there was room enough, he thrust his head and shoulders through and then pulled himself out and stood up, dusting himself off — and found he was facing not Bill Katrishen or one of his sons, but Jay Mello!

"You?" he was astonished. "What brought you back?"

Jay wiped his thick hands on his jeans and looked uncomfortable.

"Never figured to bury no man alive," he said. "That was Martin's idea. Anyway, Katrishen told me what you done for Dan."

"Did he tell you I'd killed him? I'm sorry, Jay. It was him or me."

"Sure. I knowed that when he come after you. I didn't like it nohow. What I meant, well . . . you could've left him lie. You didn't need to go git help for him. I went huntin' Dan, when I found you was alive,

144

an' I figured it was like that, that he was dead. Katrishen gave me his clothes, an' I found this . . ."

It was a note, scrawled painfully, perhaps on a rifle stock or a flat rock, written no doubt, while Jim was gone for help.

Jay

   Git shet of Marten. Sandfer's all right. He's gone for hulp to Katrisshn. I'm hard hit. Sandfer shore is wite. So long, Jay, good ridin.

Dan

"I'm sorry, Jay. He was game."

"Sure." Jay Mello scowled. "It was Martin got us into this, him an' Klee Mont. We never done no killin' before . . . maybe stole a few hosses or run off a few head of cows."

"What's happened? How long was I in there?" Jim glanced at the sun.

"About five, six hours. She'll be dark soon." Mello hesitated. "I reckon I'm goin' to take out . . . light a shuck for Texas."

Sandifer thrust out his hand. "Good luck, Jay. Maybe we'll meet again."

The outlaw nodded. He stared at the ground, and then he looked up, his tough, unshaven face strangely lonely in the late-afternoon sun. "Sure wish Dan was ridin' with me. We always rode together, him an' me, since we was kids." He rubbed a hard hand over his

145

lips. "What d'you know? That girl back to Katrishen's? She put some flowers on his grave. Sure enough."

He turned and walked to his horse, swung into the saddle, and walked his horse down the trail, a somber figure captured momentarily by the sunlight before he turned away under the pines. Incongruously Jim noticed that the man's vest was split up the back, and the crown of his hat was torn.

The gray waited patiently by the brush. Jim Sandifer untied him and swung into the saddle. It was a fast ride he made back to the ranch on Iron Creek. There he swapped saddles, explaining all to Katrishen. "I'm riding," he said. "There's no room in this country for Lee Martin now."

"Want us to come?" Bill asked.

"No. They might think it was war. You stay out of it, for we want no Pleasant Valley War here. Leave it lay. I'll settle this."

He turned from the trail before he reached the B Bar, riding through the cottonwoods and sycamores along the creek. Then he rode up between the buildings and stopped beside the corral. The saddle leather creaked when he swung down, and he saw a slight movement at the corner of the corral.

"Klee? Is that you?" It was Art Dunn. "What's goin' on up at the house?"

Jim Sandifer took a long step forward. "No, Art," he said swiftly, "it's me."

Dunn took a quick step back and grabbed for his gun, but Jim was already moving, expecting him to reach. Sandifer's left hand dropped to Art's wrist, and

146

his right smashed up in a wicked uppercut to the solar plexus.

Dunn grunted and his knees sagged. Jim let go of his wrist then, and hooked sharply to the chin, hearing Dunn's teeth click as the blow smashed home. Four times more Jim hit him, rocking his head on his shoulders, then he smashed another punch to the wind and, grabbing Dunn's belt buckle, jerked his gun belt open. The belt slipped down and Dunn staggered and went to his knees. The outlaw pawed wildly, trying to get at Jim, but he was still gasping for the wind that had been knocked out of him.

The bunkhouse door opened and Sparkman stepped into the light. "What's the matter?" he asked. "What goes on?"

Sandifer called softly, and Sparkman grunted and came down off the steps. "Jim? You here? There's the devil to pay up at the house, man. I don't know what came off up there, but there was a shootin'! When we tried to go up, Mont was on the steps with a shotgun to drive us back."

"Take care of this *hombre*. I'll find out what's wrong fast enough. Where's Grimes an' Rep?"

"Rep Dean rode over to the line cabin on Cabin Creek to round up some boys in case of trouble. Grimes is inside."

"Then take Dunn an' keep your eyes open. I may need help. If I yell, come loaded for bear and hunting hair."

Jim Sandifer turned swiftly and started for the house. He walked rapidly, circling as he went toward the little-used front door, opened only on company occasions. That door, he knew, opened into a large, old-fashioned parlor that was rarely used. It was a show place, stiff and uncomfortable, and mostly gilt and plush. The front door was usually locked, but he remembered that he had occasion to help move some furniture not long before and the door had been left unlocked. There was every chance that it still was, for the room was so little used as to be almost forgotten.

Easing up on the verandah, he tiptoed across to the door and gently turned the knob. The door opened inward, and he stepped swiftly through and closed it behind him. All was dark and silent, but there was light under the intervening door and a sound of movement. With the thick carpet muffling his footfalls, he worked his way across the room to the door.

"How's the old man?" Martin was asking.

His mother replied. "He's all right. He'll live."

Martin swore. "If that girl hadn't bumped me, I'd have killed him and we'd be better off. We could easy enough fix things so that Sandifer would get blamed for it."

"Don't be in such a hurry," Rose Martin intervened. "You're always in such a fret. The girl's here, an' we can use her to help. As long as we have her, the old man will listen, and, while he's hurt, she'll do as she's told."

Martin muttered under his breath. "If we'd started by killing Sandifer like I wanted, all would be well," he said irritably. "What he said about the Katrishen trouble startin' with our comin' got the old man to

148

thinkin'. Then I figure Bowen was sorry he fired his foreman."

"No matter." Rose Martin was brusque. "We've got this place, and we can handle the Katrishens ourselves. There's plenty of time now Sandifer's gone."

Steps sounded. "Lee, the old man's comin' out of it. He wants his daughter."

"Tell him to go climb a tree," Martin replied stiffly. "You watch him."

"Where's Art?" Klee protested. "I don't like it, Lee. He's been gone too long. Somethin's up."

"Aw, forget it. Quit cryin'. You do more yelpin' than a mangy coyote."

Sandifer stood very still, thinking. There was no sound of Elaine, so she must be a prisoner in her room. Turning, he tiptoed across the room toward the far side. A door there, beyond the old piano, opened into Elaine's room. Carefully he tried the knob. It held.

At that very instant a door opened abruptly, and he saw light under the door before him. He heard a startled gasp from Elaine and Lee Martin's voice, taunting, familiar.

"What's the matter? Scared?" Martin laughed. "I just came in to see if you was all right. If you'd kept that pretty mouth of yours shut, your dad would still be all right. You tellin' him Sandifer was correct about the Katrishens an' that he shouldn't've fired him . . ."

"He shouldn't have," the girl said quietly. "If he was here now, he'd kill you. Get out of my room."

"Maybe I ain't ready to go," he taunted. "An' from now on I'm goin to come an' go as I like."

His steps advanced into the room, and Jim tightened his grip on the knob. He remembered that lock, and it was not set very securely. Suddenly an idea came to him. Turning, he picked up an old glass lamp, large and ornate. Balancing it momentarily in his hand, he drew it back and hurled it with a long overhand swing through the window.

Glass crashed on the verandah, and the lamp hit, went down a step, and stayed there. Inside the girl's room, there was a startled exclamation, and he heard running footsteps from both the girl's room and the old man's. Somebody yelled: "What's that? What happened?" And he hurled his shoulder against the door.

As he had expected, the flimsy lock carried away and he was catapulted through the door into Elaine's bedroom. Catching himself, he wheeled like a cat and sprang for the door that opened into the living room beyond. He reached it just as Mont jerked the curtain back, but, not wanting to endanger the girl, he swung hard with his fist instead of drawing his gun.

The blow came out of a clear sky to smash Mont on the jaw, and he staggered back into the room. Jim Sandifer sprang through, legs spread, hands wide.

"You, Martin," he said sharply. "Draw!"

Lee Martin was a killer, but no gunman. White to the lips, his eyes deadly, he sprang behind his mother and grabbed for the shotgun.

"Shoot, Jim!" Elaine cried. "Shoot!"

He could not. Rose Martin stood between him and his target, and Martin had the shotgun now and was swinging it. Jim lunged, shoving the table over, and the

150

lamp shattered in a crash. He fired, and then fired again. Flame stabbed the darkness at him, and he fell back against the wall, switching his gun. Fire laced the darkness into a stabbing crimson crossfire, and the room thundered with sound, and then died to stillness that was the stillness of death itself.

No sound remained, only the acrid smell of gunpowder mingled with the smell of coal oil and the faint, sickish-sweet smell of blood. His guns ready, Jim crouched in the darkness, alert for movement. Somebody groaned, and then sighed deeply, and a spur grated on the floor. From the next room, Gray Bowen called weakly: "Daughter? Daughter, what's happened? What's wrong?"

There was no movement yet, but the darkness grew more familiar. Jim's eyes became more accustomed to it. He could see no one standing. Yet it was Elaine who broke the stillness.

"Jim? Jim, are you all right? Oh, Jim . . . are you safe?" Maybe they were waiting for this.

"I'm all right," he said.

"Light your lamp, will you?"

Deliberately he moved, and there was no sound within the room, only outside, a running of feet on the hard-packed earth. Then a door slammed open, and Sparkman stood there, gun in hand.

"It's all right, I think," Sandifer said. "We shot it out."

Elaine entered the room with a light and caught herself with a gasp at the sight before her. Jim reached for the lamp.

"Go to your father," he said swiftly. "We'll take care of this."

Sparkman looked around, and was followed into the room by Grimes. "Good grief," he gasped. "They are all dead. All of them."

"The woman, too?" Sandifer's face paled. "I hope I didn't . . ."

"You didn't," Grimes said. "She was shot in the back by her own son. Shootin' in the dark, blind an' gun crazy."

"Maybe it's better," Sparkman said. "She was an old hellion."

Klee Mont had caught his right at the end of his eyebrow, and a second shot along the ribs. Sandifer walked away from him and stood over Lee Martin. His face twisted in a sneer, the dead man lay sprawled on the floor, literally shot to doll rags.

"You didn't miss many," Sparkman said grimly.

"I didn't figure to," Jim said. "I'll see the old man, and then give you a hand."

"Forget it." Grimes looked up, his eyes faintly humorous. "You stay in there. An' don't spend all your time with the old man. We need a new set-up on this here spread, an' with a new son-in-law who's a first-rate cattleman, Gray could set back an' relax."

Sandifer stopped with his hand on the curtain. "Maybe you got something there," he said thoughtfully. "Maybe you have."

"You can take my word for it," Elaine said, stepping into the door beside Jim. "He has. He surely has."